SecretsWeKeep

Share the love and laughter with three friends—
on their journey to wedded bliss....

In the breathtaking peaks of the Himalayas,
three women on the most challenging cycling
adventure of their lives are about to
share the secrets of their hearts.

They make a pact to change their lives.
And when the trip comes to an end, and the
three new friends head home to different corners
of the globe, Belle, Simone and Claire
start taking charge of their destinies....

Meet the men who will share their secrets and
bring love and laughter to the lives of these
extraordinary women.

Last month you met Belle in
Reunited: Marriage in a Million by Liz Fielding.

This month, share Simone's story in
Needed: Her Mr. Right by Barbara Hannay.

And next month, the journey ends with Claire in
Found: Her Long-Lost Husband by Jackie Braun.

*As Ryan read Simone's diary—
the diary she had asked him to
read—it was as if she were there,
revealing her secret...*

It was all very well to tell my secrets to two strangers on a
mountaintop. The real test will come if I ever fall in love.
Will I ever be able to tell that man what I've told Belle
and Claire?

I have this happy dream in my head that one day I'll
meet a man I can totally trust, and I'll be able to tell him
everything.

I know that if I'm ever able to tell him this, it will be
because I love him deeply and trust him completely.

Is it too much to hope that such a man exists?

I sit here at the top of the world and imagine I can see all
the people on Earth down below. Six billion. I only want
one. One man I can share this diary with. Just one man
who will accept me, my life, my heart.

BARBARA HANNAY

Needed: Her Mr. Right

SecretsWeKeep

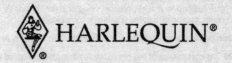

HARLEQUIN®

TORONTO • NEW YORK • LONDON
AMSTERDAM • PARIS • SYDNEY • HAMBURG
STOCKHOLM • ATHENS • TOKYO • MILAN • MADRID
PRAGUE • WARSAW • BUDAPEST • AUCKLAND

ISBN-13: 978-0-373-03976-0
ISBN-10:   0-373-03976-X

NEEDED: HER MR. RIGHT

First North American Publication 2007.

Dear Reader,

When Liz Fielding first asked me to join her in writing a trilogy with Jackie Braun, I didn't hesitate—not even for a split second. And what a wonderful journey we've been on together, from the early discussions, through all the stages of the writing process.

In much the same way, our three heroines, Belle, Simone and Claire, support each other when they return home from the Himalayas to face the challenges of their pasts. For Simone, revealing the truth about her own past is terrifying, but she's plunged into even deeper turmoil when she loses her private diary and compromises the shared secrets of her two friends.

Simone never expects to find that very special man—someone she can trust with the truth about her past, and her hopes for the future. But, as you will soon discover, her Mr. Right is just around the corner.

Warmest wishes,

Barbara

With special thanks to:

Elizabeth Heaton, my intrepid cycling sister, whose trek through the Himalayas was our inspiration.

Liz Fielding and Jackie Braun for their enthusiasm and wisdom.

My husband, Elliot, writer mate Anne Gracie and editors Meg Sleightholme and Lydia Mason, who kept me on the right track.

PROLOGUE

Simone's Diary—Day One:

ARRIVED IN BANGKOK at 10.30 p.m. Very hot and muggy. Tomorrow I enter China and I'm freaking out.

Am stressing about my fitness, wondering if the long bike rides each weekend and the daily slogs in the pool are enough preparation for cycling four hundred and fifty kilometres across the Himalayas. What if I can't keep up with the others?

Everyone at work is convinced I'm crackers. I don't expect them to understand why I need to do this, to push myself out of my comfort zone.

Problem is, tonight, I'm thinking maybe I am crazy. I mean, fundraising for street kids aside, what am I trying to prove?

It'd be nice if I came up with an answer some time in the next twelve days.

1.00 a.m. Couldn't sleep so wandered off in search of a cute little bar for a drink or a snack, got totally lost and was propositioned by a middle-aged tourist.

Arrived back here even more stressed. Still can't sleep. My hotel bed is so hard I might as well lie on the floor—the carpet and underlay are softer than this apology for a mattress.

I'm going to be tired, stressed and unfit for the start tomorrow.

Disaster!

CHAPTER ONE

*"Journeys end in lovers meeting; every wise man's
son doth know."*
William Shakespeare

JET lagged and dull headed after his long flight from
London to Sydney, Ryan Tanner was waiting in the
Customs queue when he first saw the girl with the turn-
and-stare legs.

He caught sight of her again when he was pushing
his luggage trolley through the Arrivals hall.

The slim blonde in a belted pink shift, with long
golden-brown legs and strappy high-heeled sandals,
was like a glowing hologram moving confidently
through the drab tide of travellers dressed in predictable,
look-alike business suits or denim jeans.

But Ryan's interest in her, although keen, was fleeting. Stunning as the girl was, she was a total stranger
among thousands of strangers. Ryan had no idea where
she'd come from or where she was heading. And his focus now was on getting home.

Home, after a year and a half in London. Home, after eighteen months of dreary British weather.

He'd spent a good part of the flight dreaming of sunshine and his first view of Bondi Beach—aquamarine surf breaking into white froth on yellow sand. But, with his usual lousy luck, it was pouring rain in Sydney today. The view was obscured by grey clouds.

Now, head down against the sheeting rain, he left the terminal building and felt his mood sink from travel-weary-jaded to downright morose as he steered his unwieldy trolley piled with two suitcases, a bulky snowboard and a laptop.

There was, of course, a long queue at the taxi rank.

Ryan yawned and supposed he should have let someone know he was arriving this morning. But, after a twenty hour flight, he was too tired to bother with conversation, with the inevitable questions about London and the ugly row with his Fleet Street editor.

Besides, he felt scruffy, needed a shower. And a shave wouldn't go astray, he thought, rubbing at the rough stubble on his jaw.

Then he saw the young woman again.

Fresh as a newly picked peach, she was standing ahead of him in the queue.

Wind, whipping across the street and under the awning, exposed enticing glimpses of her divine legs before she got control of her skirt.

He spent a pleasant moment wondering if she was a European tourist or an Australian coming home.

Three businessmen at the front of the queue climbed into the same taxi and Ryan shuffled forward, dragging his luggage trolley with him, pleased that the line was diminishing at a reasonable rate.

He thought about his comfortable, slightly shabby flat in Balmain and hoped that the tenants, who'd rented it while he was away, hadn't treated it too badly.

He stole another quick glance at the girl, not that he made a habit of ogling attractive girls, but this one intrigued him. He tried to pin down the quality that grabbed his attention, apart from her legs.

Perhaps it was an impression of vitality and fitness, the way she stood, shoulders back, head high, suggesting can-do confidence without conceit. Her bulky backpack surprised him. She looked the type who would travel with expensive matching suitcases.

Suddenly, almost as if she'd felt his eyes on her, she turned and looked straight at him, and for electrifying seconds their gazes met and held.

Her eyes were dark—blue or brown, he couldn't be sure—her brows darker than her hair and well defined. And, as she looked at him, he could have sworn that her mild, slightly bored expression changed.

He sensed a tiny stirring of interest from her. A ripple. The briefest flicker at the corner of her mouth. The barest beginnings of a smile.

He decided to smile back and discovered he was already smiling. Had he been grinning like a fool?

And then it happened. A tremulous, gut-punching sense of connection with this girl seized him by the throat, drove air from his lungs.

But in the next breath her taxi arrived. The driver jumped out and grabbed her pack, grumbling noisily at having to leave the warmth of his cab and splash about in the rain. The girl slipped quickly into the back passenger seat. Ryan caught one final flash of her beautiful bare legs before she shut the door.

The driver, a very glum fellow indeed, dumped her bulky backpack into the taxi's boot. He already had a couple of boxes in there and he spent a bad-tempered few minutes in the rain, shoving and cramming her pack, squeezing it mercilessly into the too small space.

At last the bulky pack was squashed enough to allow him to slam the door but, as he did, something slipped from one of the pack's side pockets and fell into the rain-filled gutter with a plop.

It was a small book.

"Hey, mister, you want this cab or not?"

Ryan turned, surprised to discover that other passengers had left and he'd reached the top of the queue. A taxi driver was scowling at him.

His eyes swivelled back to the book in the gutter. *Her* book. Small and thick with a brown leather cover of good quality. It looked like a diary or one of those fancy planners many people couldn't live without. And no one else seemed to have seen it fall.

"Just a sec." Ryan waved violently to catch her driver's attention. "Hey, you've dropped something!"

But it was too late.

The driver was already slipping behind the wheel. His door slammed and, with an impatient, throaty roar, his cab shot out from the kerb, ducked across two lanes and streaked off, leaving the girl's book lying in the rain.

"Listen, mate, you either get in this cab or step aside. You can't hold up the bloody queue in this weather."

But Ryan stared after the other cab and at the book, lying in the gutter. If it wasn't rescued quickly it would be ruined.

And why should he care?

Why should he, Ryan Tanner, a seen-it-all, done-it-all, travel-weary journalist, jeopardise his precious place in a taxi queue while he dived into pouring rain to retrieve an unknown stranger's sodden book from the gutter?

He hadn't the foggiest clue. It didn't make any sense.

But, then again, he'd always been a curious type and he'd looked into the girl's beautiful eyes...

So perhaps it made perfect sense.

Whatever...In the next unthinking, reckless split-second he grabbed his suitcase out of the driver's hands, hurled it into the taxi's boot and yelled, "We've got to follow that cab in the far lane!"

The driver's jaw gaped. "You're joking."

"Never more serious, mate." Ryan dashed for the gutter, shouting over his shoulder, "Get the other case and stow my snowboard in the back."

As he scooped up the book, he was aware of a moment's indecision behind him before the driver gave a strangely excited cry and leapt forward.

The snowboard was shoved into the back of the cab and the two men jerked their front doors open and leapt in, Ryan clutching his laptop. And the wet book.

The driver's dark eyes were flashing with high excitement as he depressed the accelerator. He turned and grinned at Ryan. "I've been waiting twenty years for a chase!"

Ahead of them, the girl's cab was still in sight—

just. It had stopped at a junction, but any second now the lights would change.

As the lights turned green, Simone wriggled her shoulders and deliberately relaxed into the luxurious hug of soft leather upholstery. She closed her eyes and tried to shrug off the sense that nothing about her homecoming felt right.

Perhaps that was what happened when you came down from the top of the world. Literally.

Three days ago, she'd been madly celebrating the achievement of a lifetime. She'd never before experienced anything like that heady feeling of supreme accomplishment—or the wonderful sense of camaraderie she'd shared with her fellow cyclists.

The trip had produced all kinds of unexpected extras...best of all the especially close bond she'd formed with her new friends, Belle and Claire...the deep sense of connection that they'd all felt up there in the mountains, far away from their everyday worlds...the trust they'd developed.

And then, near the end of the journey...the dark secrets they'd unburdened.

The pact the three women had made.

The promise.

Oh, cringe. Simone shut her eyes quickly. *Oh, help.*

Every time she thought about the terrible secret she'd revealed to Belle and Claire that night, she felt a shaft of hot, terrifying panic.

It was so hard to believe that she'd actually told them. She'd said it out loud—revealed the one thing she never talked about.

Never. To anyone.

At the time it had felt amazingly good to get it off her chest at last. A blessed relief. After all, Belle and Claire had both spilled secrets too. And they hadn't reeled back in horror at her story. She'd been lulled into thinking that perhaps it wasn't so shocking after all.

And she'd felt so happy, so strong in her brave decision to visit her grandfather at last, to break her promise to her mother and to tell him what she should have confessed years ago. To ask for his forgiveness.

But everything had seemed different when she'd been up there, in the rarefied atmosphere of the Himalayas. Her vision had been clearer, choices had appeared straightforward. It had seemed perfectly OK for three women from totally different worlds—an Aussie, a Yank and a Brit—to make life-changing decisions beneath the benevolent gaze of Jade Dragon Snow Mountain.

Now, coming home, Simone wasn't so sure. Sharing her secret had changed everything, complicated everything.

Before, no one else in the world knew, and she could almost convince herself that the events on that terrible night her stepfather died had never really occurred.

Now, she was frightened. She wished Belle and Claire weren't so far away. She needed their reassurance that her life wasn't going to collapse because they *knew*.

They'd agreed to stay in touch, to share regular emails and to help each other through the weeks ahead. Simone hoped that would be enough. She felt so…so…anxious. And something else. What was it? Not depressed exactly. Deflated? Yeah…definitely. She felt flat. Very flat.

* * *

They'd lost sight of the girl's taxi.

Despite Ryan's driver's most valiant attempts, there was simply too much traffic, too much rain and too many taxis zipping back and forth. They'd had to admit defeat.

Now, as his taxi dashed through Sydney's rain-lashed streets, heading for his flat in Balmain, the diary sat on the seat beside Ryan. The thick leather cover had saved it from a soaking and a few shakes and a wipe on his jeans had rendered it almost as good as new.

But so far Ryan hadn't been able to identify the book's owner.

Funny how much that bothered him.

His fingers drummed on the leather cover as he stared ahead at the frantic motion of the windscreen wipers. Under other circumstances he might have tracked back to the terminal and handed the diary in to the airport's lost property office.

But he was dog-tired, it was lousy weather and they had already been halfway across Sydney before they'd given up the chase and before he'd realised that the pretty blonde had not filled in the personal information page inside the book's front cover.

Of course he hadn't rescued her book simply to discover her name, address and telephone number. It was more a sense of fair play that had sent him diving into the gutter. But now he was left in something of a quandary. He had no idea who she was. And he realised, too late, that was the way she wanted it.

Why else would she keep a diary without including any personal contact details?

This diary, with its closely written pages, was nothing

like the small, dog-eared notepad filled with scribbled contacts, appointments, story leads and notes that Ryan kept in his inner coat pocket.

He'd thumbed through a few pages and read enough to realise that this was a very personal record, meant for her eyes only—a mixture of internal musings as well as a detailed account of a recent bike ride through the Himalayas.

Himalayas? Wow, no wonder she looked fit.

She'd begun writing in neat black ink, but she must have lost the pen halfway through the trip and the rest of the pages were written in a mixture of red ballpoint and blunt pencil.

Ryan flicked the book's pages once more and they fell open in the middle, where she'd wedged postcards—a Buddhist temple, towering snow capped mountains, Chinese villagers in traditional dress, a breathtaking view down a gorge. He checked the back of each postcard to see if any had been addressed, but they were blank.

Frustrated, he closed the book again.

And decided he wouldn't read it.

OK, so he was a journalist and journalists were noted for sticking their noses into other people's business. He'd been doing exactly that in the UK for the past eighteen months—until his recent, rather notorious departure.

Now, he'd come home to regroup, to think about new directions. The last thing he needed was a scavenger hunt, digging through an innocent young woman's personal journal for pay dirt.

Besides, he'd stood in that taxi queue and looked into her eyes.

And somehow that made a difference.

Anyway…a cycling holiday in China was hardly breaking news.

That settled, he slipped the diary into his pocket and turned his attention to familiar Sydney landmarks. He was almost home.

For Simone, the single best thing about coming home was her lovely modern apartment in Newtown.

She'd invested in this soon after she'd landed her plum job as executive editor of *City Girl* magazine. Spacious and open-plan, great for parties and handy for the *City Girl* offices, it suited her lifestyle perfectly.

She loved everything about it, from the lively purple feature wall in the living room and the mezzanine level that housed her home office and bedroom, to the funky retro-style stools lined up at the kitchen counter—a favourite gathering spot for her friends.

Today, however, as she set her key in the lock, she didn't feel quite the sense of welcome that she'd hoped for. Ever since she'd farewelled Belle and Claire at Hong Kong airport, a vague sense of unease seemed to have taken root inside her.

Silly. She wasn't going to sink into gloom. All she needed was to kick off the designer sandals she'd splurged on in Hong Kong—gorgeous, but still a tad uncomfortable—and she would make a nice hot cup of tea and reread some of the affirmations she'd written in her diary when she'd felt so fantastic up in the mountains.

Barefoot, she padded across the timber floor to her backpack and she looked down at it, rubbing at her forehead as she tried to remember where she'd packed the diary. It was in one of the outside pockets.

She rolled the pack a little, patting the pockets, to feel their contents. Toiletries in this one. Her camera in this other, a small bottle of French perfume from the duty free and—

No!

A jolt ripped through her as she felt the unmistakable flatness of an empty pocket. Her heart began to race. There shouldn't be any empty pockets in her pack. She'd crammed her possessions into every available space.

This pocket was where she kept—

Frantically, she checked the other pockets, hoping against hope to find a familiar rectangular shape.

It wasn't there.

"Oh, no!" Her cry was almost a wail. "I don't believe it!"

She'd put her diary in this pocket. And it was gone. Stooping closer, she saw that the zip was broken. Her heart jerked erratically as she traced it with her fingers and found an irregular gap in the metal teeth. Fighting a growing sense of panic, she tried to remember when it could have happened. She could distinctly remember seeing the reassuring book-shaped bulge of her diary in this pocket when she'd gone through Customs.

Groaning, she thought of everything she'd written— her faithful descriptions of every point of the journey through China, the scenery, the cycling, the aches and pains, triumphs and fears…

The secrets!

Oh, cringe. What if someone read *them?*

She hadn't merely written the outpourings of her own heart, she'd included the secrets that Belle and Claire had shared too. And she'd written down details of the private pact they'd made.

She covered her face with her hands. Panic threatened.

Fighting it, she forced herself to remember everything she'd done at the airport, retraced her steps in her mind…getting through Security, pushing her pack on a trolley through the Arrivals hall, waiting outside, locking eyes with the hot guy in the taxi queue. The tall, smiling guy with the stubble and the amazing dark brown eyes that—

Oh, give it a miss, Simone. As if he's relevant!

She gave an impatient cry of self-recrimination.

She couldn't lose her diary. She just couldn't! Apart from the dire possibility that she was scattering her new friends' secrets to the four winds, she was writing an article for *City Girl* about the trip and she needed the notes she'd made.

Thank heavens she'd emailed a fairly comprehensive coverage of her journey through from Hong Kong to her office yesterday, which meant she'd still be able to write the article, even without her diary. It was the personal stuff in there that sent her stomach churning.

And now some stranger might—

She jumped to her feet as she remembered the awful thump when the taxi driver had dumped the pack into the boot of the car. The whole vehicle had rocked with the force of it. Maybe it had fallen out into the boot.

Perhaps her driver had already turned it in to the taxi company's lost property. She could phone them, ask all their drivers to check their vehicles…offer a reward.

Excited by fresh hope, she rushed to her telephone.

Ryan piled his suitcases, snowboard and laptop in the middle of his living room and looked about him. It felt strange to come home to his flat after so long away.

Professional cleaners had been in and left the place super-tidy and smelling of artificial room freshener and disinfectant. Devoid of character.

Sad truth was, his home didn't really feel like home without a fine layer of dust over the furniture and a scattering of newspapers, books and at least three dirty coffee mugs.

He yawned again—a jet lag induced yawn so huge he almost cracked his jaw.

He needed a coffee.

Damn. With a groan, he realised that his cupboards were bare. The tenants hadn't left anything—even the sugar bowl was empty.

To add to his annoyance, his mobile phone rang.

Ryan almost ignored it but, a split-second before it rang out, he relented and answered.

"Hello?"

"So you're home son."

"Hi, Dad." Ryan's stomach sank. An interrogation from JD the minute he arrived home was the last thing he needed. "I've just walked in the door."

"So, what are your plans now? Now that the London venture's fallen through."

Fallen through? The old man had such a sweet turn of phrase—and an incredible capacity for ignoring the facts. As if JD didn't know that it was his insensitive interference from the other side of the world that had forced Ryan's resignation.

"Uh—I haven't made any definite plans yet, Dad. I'm going to take a little time out. To regroup."

"Regroup? What kind of rubbish is that? You need a plan, Ryan. A business plan. That's your problem, you know."

You're my problem, Ryan almost snapped. His father couldn't leave him alone. But if he told JD that, he'd leave himself wide open for a tirade.

He got one anyway.

"It's high time you did something about your lifestyle, Ryan. You're still drifting aimlessly. No focus. No goal. You're past thirty, son, and still a hack journalist."

For crying out loud.

"You know you should be in management by now. Running budgets, hiring and firing."

Ryan held the receiver away from his ear as his father rattled on.

"I've had an idea that might suit you," JD said. "It's time you used the money in the trust fund your mother left you. Use it to buy up a little country newspaper. You would get one for a song. Get it up and running and then knock off the other papers in the region. Build quite a good business."

Ryan groaned softly. "Thanks for the suggestion, but I've no intention of burying myself in some sleepy country town."

"But for—"

"Dad, I'm taking a short break and then I'm going to concentrate on specialist writing. Features. Human interest. I'll look up some of my old contacts at *The Sydney Chronicle*."

"Surely you're not going to crawl back to the rag where you started?"

"I can and I shall. I'm very happy with my life." Ryan's voice rose several decibels. "OK?"

He disconnected, felt drained. In recent years, hanging up in mid-conversation had been the only way to avoid an almighty argument with his father.

I'm very happy with my life.

It was almost true.

And that was more than JD could claim. His father might be an Australian success story, but he was into his third marriage and was still obsessed with wiping out his business opponents. Ryan couldn't imagine ever finding pleasure from that.

JD owned a string of iron ore and gold mines and several cattle stations, a mansion in Perth, an apartment overlooking Sydney Harbour, an island in the Great Barrier Reef and a villa on the Côte d'Azur, but his billions had never bought him the kind of contentment that Ryan longed for.

Nevertheless, in his father's eyes Ryan would always be a failure. Christopher, the elder son, was the Good Son, the golden child. He'd followed in JD's footsteps, had acquired a Ph.D. in mining engineering, a beautiful trophy wife and two fine sons.

Ryan was the black sheep.

Most of the time he didn't let it bother him. And yet…

He felt strangely alone.

Like a congenital defect, loneliness had dogged him since childhood, since he'd first known he would never bask in the warmth of his father's approval.

And right now he was tired. Physically and emotionally. But he knew from experience that it was best after a long international flight to grit it out until night time before hitting the hay.

He really needed coffee.

With not a coffee bean in sight, he opted for Plan B. He would head for Stratos's café. He could spend the afternoon there, surrounded by Sydneysiders, drinking endless cups of coffee.

Picking up his coat, he felt the weight of the girl's book in the pocket.

He felt the grain of the leather cover beneath his fingers and then, as he took the diary out and set it on the bookcase, he thought about its owner. Remembered her tentative smile, her lovely eyes.

He should do something about getting this back to her. But the conversation with his father had destroyed his sense of gallantry.

Maybe tomorrow. Right now, he needed coffee.

CHAPTER TWO

SIMONE couldn't sleep for worrying about her diary, couldn't believe she'd lost it. She'd called the cab company but there was no report anywhere of it being handed in. She was terribly afraid that the diary had disappeared for ever.

But where was it? Had someone found it? Would they bother to read it? Would they ever link it to her?

The cab company had asked her to leave her name and a contact number, but she'd been too afraid to reveal her identity. What if her story was leaked to the press?

The possibilities tossed around and around in her head like debris swirling down a drainpipe and finally she gave up trying to sleep. Slipping out of bed, she padded in bare feet through the dark flat to her study, blinked at the brightness as her computer screen came to life and read Belle and Claire's emails for the zillionth time.

Belle had written:

Oh, Simone! What a shame about your diary. I know how hard you worked on it—will you be able to put together your article without it? If you need any details, I've got the stuff I wrote for my reports that you can have. As for anyone connecting us with it, I wouldn't worry too much. It's most likely in some airport waste compactor by now.

That was a comforting thought. If only she could believe it.

Claire had been equally sympathetic and reassuring:

Don't beat yourself up about this. It's disappointing and frustrating, but I can't imagine it will cause any problems for any of us.

Simone closed down her email programme, hoping the girls were right. It wouldn't be so bad if she hadn't included so many personal ramblings in her diary. She hadn't meant to get deep and meaningful. Her intention had been simply to record the cycling challenge, but for years now she'd kept her inner self so tightly under wraps that once she was out of the country and had started to write, all kinds of thoughts, hopes and fears had tumbled on to the page.

So many dreams and dreads, memories and secrets...

Up there in the Himalayas, close beneath the stars, she'd looked at the vast dome of sky and hadn't been able to stop thinking about her parents. Both dead. She'd never known her father—he'd died before she was born, fighting in Vietnam. Her mother had died when she was seventeen.

She'd thought a great deal about her grandfather, who was very much alive, although she hadn't seen him in over a decade.

Belle and Claire had been going through something similar, she'd discovered later, which was why they'd eventually made their pact and why Simone had pledged to go to Jonathan Daintree, her grandfather, to tell him what she should have told him years ago.

But now, back in Sydney and sitting alone in the dark, her courage seemed to have abandoned her totally.

In the eerie darkness, her eyes sought the familiar shape of an old cardboard box on the bookshelf beside her. It held all the Christmas and birthday cards her grandfather had sent her. Each card had come with a generous cheque and she'd written polite notes to thank him, but on both sides their correspondence had been guarded and coldly polite for some time now.

And it was her fault.

After her mother's death, she'd distanced herself from the old man. At first there had been occasional fleeting meetings in cafés when Jonathan had come to town. A kiss on the cheek…

A handful of words…

"How are you?"

"I'm fine, thanks, Grandfather."

"You know you're always welcome at Murrawinni."

"Yes, but I'm so busy."

She'd had to force the distance between them. It was awful and she knew she'd broken his heart, but if she'd remained close with Jonathan he would have asked too many questions. Questions about her stepfather, Harold Pearson's, death, about her mother Angela's involvement. Questions Simone could never answer.

Her mother had begged her never to tell anyone.

But could her mother have guessed the unbearable burden that ban had imposed?

Living with such a terrible secret had not only soured her relationship with her grandfather; her refusal to talk about it was at the root of her string of broken relationships with men. For Simone, the whole getting-to-know-you dating scene was fraught with tension.

Each time she went out with a new boyfriend, she always hoped that this would be *The One*. She would give anything to fall completely, obsessively, permanently in love with one wonderful man, but the burden of her secret always held her back.

In the Himalayas, she had come to the alarming decision that Angela had been wrong to silence her. The guilty secret had blighted her life and the pain of separation from her grandfather was too great. She owed him the truth.

And now she had to find the courage to tell him everything. And she had to do it fast, because—*oh, help*—because the person who found the diary might let her secrets out and her grandfather would, most definitely, *never* forgive her then.

Simone felt her eyes sting, couldn't bring herself to look at the other larger box that held letters from her mother. Just looking at it brought a rush of painful memories and a wave of guilt and fear. She bit down hard on her lip to stop herself from crying, turned on her desk lamp and began to type a bravely hopeful reply to Belle and Claire.

* * *

Next morning, stomach churning, she dialed Murrawinni's number before she lost her nerve. Her grandfather's housekeeper, Connie Price, answered.

"I beg your pardon?" she said. "Who did you say is calling?"

"Simone. Simone Gray, Jonathan's granddaughter."

"Simone?" Connie's voice quavered with surprised disbelief. "Lord have mercy, child. This is going to be quite a shock for him. It's been so long."

Simone's stomach lurched. "Is my grandfather well? I don't want to upset him or make him ill."

"I don't think there's any fear of that, Simone. He's well enough. Fit as a fiddle, in fact. Keeps us all on our toes. Just a moment and I'll fetch him."

Connie took more than a moment and Simone's heart accelerated to a gallop while she waited. Would her grandfather be angry? Would he refuse to speak to her? Would he hammer her with a thousand questions?

"Simone?" It was Connie's voice again.

"Yes?"

"I—I'm sorry, my dear. Jonathan—" Connie paused and cleared her throat. "I'm afraid he can be a little stubborn these days."

"What does that mean? Are you saying that he doesn't want to speak to me?" Simone's voice broke pitifully. She screwed her face tight, fighting tears. "I was hoping to ask if I could come out to Murrawinni to—to visit him. Th-there's something I need—"

She broke off, couldn't get the words out.

"I'm sure he'll come round, dear. It's just that your call has been quite a shock. It's been such a long time."

"Yes." The word came out as a despairing squeak. "Perhaps Grandfather will ring me l-later, if—if he changes his mind."

Simone gave Connie her number and hung up, felt an overwhelming sense of defeat. She'd already lost her diary. What else could go wrong?

By the end of a few days of self-imposed vacation, the printer's ink in Ryan's veins drove him back to *The Sydney Chronicle* newsroom. He was greeted with flattering enthusiasm and predictable curiosity about the row that had ended his time in London.

"What was that about?" asked Jock Guinness, the chief-of-staff and Ryan's former mentor. "Brash young Aussie clashes with ultra-conservative British establishment?"

"More like—Aussie black sheep spits the dummy when intrusive, cashed-up father tries to jump his boy up the British promotion queue."

Jock's jaw gaped. "Your dad did that?"

Ryan's lip curled. "Who else?"

Everyone in the newsroom expected Ryan to resume his old post. The chief-of-staff announced openly that a desk could be cleared for him in ten minutes flat. But Ryan shook his head. He wasn't looking for another spot as a general news gatherer. He'd had a gutful of being sent out on tame stories pulled off the daily job sheet.

Jock accepted this with grudging good grace. "You'll do well as a freelancer," he admitted. "You were one of the few people in this place who always had a string of good stories on the back burner."

Ryan was chatting to Meg James, one of the journalists, when he saw the girl from the airport.

He stared at her picture, smiling up at him from the pages of a glossy magazine—a full-page colour photo of her, sitting cross-legged on a grassy slope with a spectacular rocky gorge behind her and snow-capped mountains in the distance. Felt again that gut-punching sensation.

He had rung the airport's lost property office, but no one had reported a missing diary. And now, here was the girl. She was wearing slim-fitting bike shorts, revealing her legs in all their shapely, golden-tanned loveliness.

He remembered the way she'd caught his attention at the airport—as if she were in glowing Technicolor and the rest of the scene was in black and white. Remembered the uncanny moment of connection when he'd locked gazes with her. Thought of the crowded handwritten pages of her diary, still sitting on his bookshelf. It was the weirdest feeling, almost as if he knew her and he'd let her down somehow.

With admirable restraint, he refrained from snatching up the magazine. Instead, he pointed to the open pages with an excessively casual hook of his right thumb. "Do you mind if I borrow this?"

Meg James shot him a curious smile. "Be my guest. But since when have you been a fan of *City Girl?*"

"I'd just like to check out this story. About the bike ride in the Himalayas."

"Oh, sure, it's a great travel piece." Meg glanced at the picture and rolled her eyes. "Simone puts the rest of us to shame."

Simone. He repeated her name softly, savouring it,

letting it settle inside him. It was a sensuous name—just a little exotic—a good fit for her.

"Simone Gray," he said, reading her byline.

"Yep. Don't you know her? She's the Big Chief at *City Girl*. Executive editor."

"No kidding?" A pulse began to throb in his jaw and fine pinpricks erupted over his arms. "Tell me more about her."

Meg sighed. "I get pea-green just thinking about Simone Gray. She's smart, successful, has the job I've always lusted after. And every time I see her, she seems to have a different guy in tow and they're all madly in love with her, of course. And then, to cap it off, instead of just writing a cheque for her favourite charity, she put herself through a huge ordeal, training hard, getting sweaty and blistered and making the rest of us feel like lazy layabouts."

Ryan set the magazine down abruptly and Meg frowned at him.

"Changed your mind about reading it?"

"Thanks, but I think I'll get what I want firsthand."

Meg treated him to a very weird look, but he was already halfway out of the office.

Simone had given her PA the day off because it was her elderly mother's birthday, so when the phone rang for the twentieth or maybe fortieth time that morning, her response was automatic. "Good morning. Simone Gray speaking. How can I help you?"

"Morning, Simone. My name's Ryan Tanner. I'm a fellow journalist and I've rung to congratulate you on the article in this month's *City Girl*. I really enjoyed your story about China. Nice work."

Simone frowned. Her article was workmanlike and professional, possibly inspiring for some readers, but not exactly the kind of writing that would attract attention from fellow journalists—especially a male with a beautifully modulated, deeply sexy voice.

He'd said his name was Tanner...Ryan Tanner...

She didn't think she'd met him, but couldn't be sure. The only Tanners she could think of offhand were billionaires who owned vast tracts of mining land in Western Australia and the Northern Territory. No one in that family would want to work as a journalist.

"Thank you, Mr Tanner. It's kind of you to take the trouble to call me."

"No trouble."

She waited a beat.

"But there is something else, Simone..."

He paused again and in the silence she decided there was something undeniably sexy about the way he said her name—warming it with his voice, touching a chord deep inside her.

It occurred to her that if this guy was as smooth as his voice suggested, he might be going to ask her on a date. He wouldn't be the first man to make contact after seeing her photo in a magazine. Her mind raced ahead, planning a quick exit strategy.

Ryan Tanner's deep voice rumbled silkily down the phone line. "I have something of yours that I'd like to return."

"Something of mine?"

"You lost a book at the airport last week."

A blast of fear exploded in her chest.

Crash.

The phone receiver slipped from her hand, clattered on to her desk.

"Simone?"

Her vital organs collided. She'd convinced herself that her precious diary had been dumped by a sullen taxi driver, or had been swept up and pulped by one of those noisy street sweeping machines. Last week, she'd rung the taxi company countless times with no luck and had decided it was safe enough to publish the Himalayan article. Had decided that even if someone had found the diary, the chances of that person reading *City Girl* and putting two and two together were negligible.

But now, only one day after *City Girl* had hit the news-stands, her worst fears were realised.

And of all people to have found the diary and make the connection, it had to be another journalist!

Her hand shook as she picked up the receiver again and held it to her ear.

"Ms Gray, are you there?"

She didn't answer.

"Ms Gray, are you OK?"

Ryan Tanner sounded concerned, but she didn't trust him.

Her mind raced in crazy panicking circles. His faux admiration of her article was a front, of course. The only reason he'd rung was to let her know he had the diary.

The sickening question was: what else did this guy know about her? And how did he plan to use it? Her stomach heaved and sweat trickled down her back as she imagined her diary entries and her innermost secret fears splashed across some grubby tabloid newspaper. Ridiculously, she even pictured her story flashed on a television news bulletin. Nausea rose from the pit of her stomach.

She had to get a grip, had to think like an editor, not a panicking victim. It was time to think in terms of crisis management.

As calmly as she could, she said, "Tell me one thing, Mr Tanner. We're not on air, are we?"

"Of course not. There's no need to panic. I only work with print media."

A huff of relief escaped her. "OK...Ryan Tanner...I'm trying to remember if I've seen your byline."

"Used to be with *The Sydney Chronicle*, but I've been in London for the last year and a half."

"And you believe you have something that belongs to me?"

"You must know what I'm talking about, Simone. Your diary."

Thinking fast now, she realised she had to play for time, needed space to think, to work out a suitable response.

"Mr Tanner—uh—Ryan, I have people queuing up in the office here. I'll have to call you back. Say in fifteen minutes?"

"OK, no problem." He gave her his number.

"This is your private number?"

"Mine and only mine."

Dropping the receiver, she sank back into her chair,

cowered with shock for a second or two, then jumped to her feet and began to pace the office, her mind racing at a hundred miles an hour. What could she do? How on earth was she going to handle this nightmare?

There was only one answer: *very carefully.*

She wished she knew how her diary had ended up in Ryan Tanner's hands. Had someone sold it to him? How many people had read it?

Fighting panic, she tried to unscramble her thoughts. She had committed the sordid details of her secret to paper and she'd exposed Belle and Claire too. And she'd recorded the pact she'd made with Belle and Claire—their commitments to find important people from their past, to right past wrongs.

How could she have been so thoughtless? So careless?

Oh, help.

Oh, hell!

Keep calm, girl.

Yes, she had to stay calm. If she kept her head, she might be able to find a way to deflect Ryan Tanner, to wriggle out of this. But she had to handle things very carefully, had to get him answering her questions, not the other way round.

She waited twenty-seven minutes, twenty-seven nerve-racking, nail-biting, agonising minutes before she rang him back.

"Hello, Mr Tanner."

Her heart thumped so loudly it filled her ears and she could hardly hear his reply.

"Simone, thanks for calling back."

"I'm rather busy, so I can't speak for long, but I do

appreciate your willingness to return my lost property."
Cringe. She sounded way too prim and uptight. She
tried again, more casually. "Perhaps you could drop the
book off at our front desk? Any time that's convenient
would be fine."

"Well…Simone."

She did her best to ignore the totally annoying
coiling sensation deep inside her when he said her
name, warming it with his dark midnight voice.

"There are a couple of things I'd like to speak to
you about."

"I'm sorry, Mr Tanner. I'm not interested in talking to
you. Certainly not before I verify that this book is mine."

"It's yours, Simone."

She clenched the receiver so tightly it should have
snapped in two.

Ryan Tanner could be planning anything—even
blackmail.

"How—" Her voice came out squeaky and scared.
She paused, tried again. "How did the diary come into
your possession?"

"Rainy day. Sydney Airport. Lovely girl waiting
for a taxi. A backpack with a side pocket. Any of that
ring a bell?"

Simone stifled a cry. This guy had been there? He'd
been watching her at the airport?

Her frantic fingers twisted the phone cord. Was he
stalking her?

She thought of the hot-looking guy she'd caught
checking her out. Surely he wasn't Tanner? He hadn't
looked like a stalker.

"So…so what are you saying, Mr Tanner—Ryan? You want to meet?"

"Why not? What about lunch?"

She needed more time, needed to find out as much as she could about this guy. "I—I'm busy today. How about tomorrow? Can we meet somewhere tomorrow?"

"Why wait? Couldn't you make time today?"

She sighed. Perhaps it would be better to meet him; otherwise he might track her to her home. Best to get this over, to be rid of him.

Her throat was dry and she swallowed. "All right. Where do you want to meet?"

"How about the Jade Dragon restaurant in Chinatown? Unless you're tired of Chinese?"

"I'll be there at one."

CHAPTER THREE

RYAN felt unusually on edge as he headed for Chinatown.

Had Simone Gray cast a spell on him?

How else could he explain why he'd invited her to lunch rather than taking the simple option of sticking her diary in the post or dropping it off at *City Girl*'s front desk?

How else could he explain his need to see her, to check again exactly why she'd stood out from the thousands of travellers at the airport?

In the photo in *City Girl*, her pretty eyes were sparkling, her mouth curved with laughter. He'd been entranced. Seeing a picture of her was like hearing a teasing scrap of enchanting music. He wanted to hear the whole song.

Under other circumstances, he might have gone out of his way to impress her at this meeting. Flashiest restaurant in town. Top wines. Waiter primed to fuss over her.

But she was already in panic mode and Ryan suspected that kind of carry-on would only make her more suspicious. Besides, it wasn't really his style.

As he passed through the traditional paifang gate into Sydney's busy, bustling Chinatown, he caught the tempting aromas of lemon grass, ginger and chilli rising from woks and he felt strangely nervous about this meeting—almost first date nervous.

Crazy, given his age and his track record with women, and the fact that, as far as she was concerned, this was so not a date.

He reached the Jade Dragon, stepped out of the sunlight into its darkened interior and took a moment for his eyes to adjust.

Simone was already there, seated at a small table on the far side, facing the entrance. A red lantern cast a rosy glow over her, illuminating the shock of recognition in her eyes.

She remembered. Remembered that fleeting moment last week when they'd locked gazes at the airport.

A tiny rocket of hope launched inside him, but it was quickly doused, as her surprised disbelief changed to clear disappointment, then displeasure.

Not the best of beginnings.

Nevertheless, he smiled as he made his way to her, kept smiling as he held out his hand.

"Hello, Simone."

She ignored his attempt to be friendly, simply looked up at him with wary eyes and a tight, no-nonsense mouth. He took the seat opposite her.

Forgot to breathe.

Close up, she was even lovelier than he'd remembered—in spite of her aloofness. Her face, framed by waves of soft, wheat-gold hair, was classically oval and beautifully symmetrical. And there was a breath-robbing quality about her perfect skin, the delicacy of her nose and mouth, the vividness of her eyes—deeply blue and darkly lashed.

She was simply dressed, but the very simplicity of her pale blue dress and the fine gold chain about her neck served as a perfect foil for her beauty. The dress showed off her golden tan to perfection. It took every ounce of self-restraint to refrain from telling her straight out that she was, quite possibly, the loveliest woman he'd ever met.

How crazy would that be? The frost and wariness in her eyes were enough to assure Ryan that Simone Gray wouldn't give a flying fig.

Angling for a safe opening, he asked, "Have you ever eaten here before?"

"No." She didn't return his smile. "But I've checked out the menu and it looks OK."

"So you're ready to order?"

She nodded.

He beckoned to a waiter and Simone ordered fish in black bean sauce. Ryan chose Mongolian lamb. They both skipped the wine list and ordered jasmine tea.

In a matter of moments the waiter was gone and they were alone again.

Across the table their gazes met and Ryan caught the tiniest flare of interest in her eyes, but it was so quickly doused, like a hastily snuffed candle, that he decided he'd imagined it.

He cleared his throat. "I genuinely meant what I said about your travel piece in *City Girl*. I really liked it. I've been on the Nepalese side of the Himalayas, but not in China, and I think you definitely captured the atmosphere of the region. It's a fine piece of writing—conveyed a great sense of immediacy, of being there with you."

Her right eyebrow lifted. "Mr Tanner—"

"Simone." He offered her his most charming smile. "I'm sure you can force yourself to call me Ryan."

She blinked, then managed a stiff quarter-smile. "Ryan, we both know I'm not here for a literary critique." Sitting back, with her slim hands folded in front of her, she studied him grimly. "And I'm sure you'll agree that my story might have had a greater sense of immediacy, not to mention accuracy, if I'd been able to consult my diary."

He shrugged. "You made it rather difficult for me to return it. There were absolutely no contact details."

She dismissed this with an impatient wave of her hand. "I didn't expect to lose it. I'm always exceptionally careful."

"I'm sure you are."

She shot him a narrow look as if she suspected he was teasing her.

"Unfortunately," he added, "your taxi driver wasn't so careful."

Simone's eyes widened.

"The diary fell out while he was cramming your backpack into the boot."

"I thought something like that must have happened. I rang the cab company, but no one handed it in."

Ryan sighed. "I rang the airport lost property, but no one had listed any contact details for a lost diary."

Tense silence fell as she sat watching him, challenging him with her deep, blue, disapproving eyes. "You did bring it, didn't you?"

No point in playing games. Ryan took the book out of his coat pocket and set it on the table.

Her mouth tightened as she stared at it. "I suppose you've read every word."

"As a matter of fact, I haven't."

She shot him a sharp, doubtful look, bristling with disbelief, and then, with an impatient cry, she reached for the book. Almost instinctively Ryan's hand closed over hers. Why? He couldn't quite explain.

Simone gasped and Ryan felt a fine tremor pass through her, through him. She dropped her gaze and he saw the thick half-moons of her lashes and the faint golden-brown dusting of colour on her eyelids, the pink gloss on her lips.

"Why don't you believe me, Simone?"

She wouldn't look at him.

He persisted. "If our roles were reversed, would you have read my diary?"

For a split second she looked up, her blue eyes momentarily bewildered, shining with a suspect sheen. Her pink mouth tightened. "Why do you want to know that? Do you keep a diary?"

"No," he admitted. "But that's not the point."

For the first time she smiled, but her smile was cool and intensely sceptical. "I think the point is that you're trying to sidetrack me with hypothetical arguments."

Sighing, he let go of her hand. It was very clear that it didn't matter what he said; she would never believe him, had no intention of trusting him. Crazy how much that bothered him.

Simone pulled the diary across the table towards her, flipped through its pages, casting frantic glances here and there, and then snapped it shut. Looked worried.

Their meals arrived and she put the diary in her handbag and busied herself pouring green tea into tiny white cups for both of them. The food looked delicious, smelled divine.

Hoping to defuse the tension, Ryan picked up his chopsticks and clicked them together. "I guess you're an expert at using these now."

Ignoring him, Simone stabbed her sticks nervously into her fish. "I think I've lost my appetite."

"Take it easy, Simone. I'm not here to drag a story out of you."

She shot him a doubtful, dark-lashed glance. "Don't, for one moment, imagine you can charm it out of me."

"Wouldn't dream of anything so low."

"Then why are you here? Why couldn't you have simply dropped the diary off at my office?"

"I wanted to meet you."

She lifted a sceptical eyebrow.

Ryan shrugged and offered the fail-safe smile that worked on every female he'd ever known, from old ladies to three-year-olds. "This food smells great. Let's enjoy it."

"I can't eat." She looked suddenly pale and pushed her bowl to one side. "Let's not play games. Give it to me straight. You did read my diary and now you're after more details. You're going to print my story, aren't you?"

So there *was* a story.

Ryan couldn't help being intrigued. But he tried to reassure her. "I don't know what you're talking about."

With a huff of impatience, Simone stood, collected her handbag.

Ryan jumped to his feet. She couldn't leave now. The food smelled sensational.

She motioned for him to sit. "Enjoy your lunch. It's on me."

"That's not necessary. You're overreacting. Surely we can talk about this, Simone."

But she'd already turned and, with her back very straight, she marched across the restaurant to the front desk, handed the cashier her credit card.

Stunned, Ryan was slow to follow her, was only halfway through the maze of tables when she turned again and sent him a *look*.

Other diners were watching them and Simone's look was defiant, hard and sharp enough to cut Ryan in two.

Another step and he'd create a public spectacle. Damn. He'd really stuffed this, and chasing after her now would serve no purpose.

Lifting his hand in a curt half-salute, he flashed a final smile, turned and walked casually back to his table.

He lunched alone, without enjoyment, knowing all the time that Ms Gray had made a right royal fool of him.

But what it pointed to, of course, was the inescapable fact that there was something in her diary that was more dangerous and more distressing than he'd realised.

She was frightened of him.

Simone was still shaking when she got back to the office.

Closing her door, she collapsed into her chair with the diary clutched to her chest. She felt ill—and annoyed with herself for getting frightened and running away like that. But she'd been rattled from the moment Ryan Tanner had arrived at the restaurant and she'd realised he was the same guy she'd seen in the taxi queue at the airport!

She'd felt shocked and foolish. Last week she'd thought he was smiling at her, and she'd actually smiled back. In reality, Tanner was more likely to have been smirking than smiling. And she'd been silly enough to think he was hot-looking.

What an idiot she was!

Since when had she been taken in by a hot body, a suntan and soulful brown eyes? She let out a long, exhausted sigh. At least she had the diary now. And Ryan Tanner hadn't followed her.

It was a hollow victory.

Tanner might not have come after her, but that didn't mean he wouldn't publish her story—or Belle's and Claire's stories for that matter.

Oh, cringe.

With an angry little cry, she reached down and opened the bottom drawer of her desk, dropped the diary into it and then locked it, slipped the key into a pocket inside her handbag.

Then she swivelled in her chair to face her desktop computer. She had to send emails to Belle and Claire. To confess what had happened and to warn them.

Would they ever forgive her?

Next morning brought no relief for Simone. She stared at her computer screen and felt so on edge her teeth almost severed her lower lip. She'd spent a restless, sleepless night, racked with dread. She scanned this morning's newspapers and could find no sign of a story about her, but she knew it wouldn't be long before Ryan Tanner published everything.

How would she ever survive? What would her friends and colleagues think of her? Her grandfather?

She would try ringing Murrawinni again to warn her grandfather, but just thinking about his reaction roused a frantic mass of butterflies in her stomach.

And, to make matters worse, she had to worry about Belle and Claire too. Overnight, emails had arrived from them and, although both girls had been remarkably cool and very understanding, not blaming her at all for losing her diary, she knew they were worried.

Claire had written:

I can't say I'm happy to know my dirty laundry will soon be hanging out to dry on the public line, but I certainly don't blame you, Simone.

It's not your fault that jerk has decided to make a name for himself at our expense. Don't beat yourself up over it. If anyone deserves a good thrashing, it would be Ryan Tanner.

In the meantime, I can't keep waiting for Ethan to return my phone calls. I think a little trip is in order.

Belle had been equally sympathetic.

But, although her friends were kind and supportive, Simone knew they were upset. There was no way they wouldn't be. They were both high profile women, sure to attract huge media attention if their stories were leaked to their local press. The girls would be mortified! Belle's career as a breakfast show host would be ruined. Claire's famous family would be outraged.

And, perhaps even more importantly, if the beans about their Himalayan pacts were spilled, their missions would be in jeopardy. She mustn't allow that to happen. Belle really, really needed to track down her sister, Daisy, and Claire desperately wanted to find Ethan, her ex-husband.

Simone couldn't let the loss of her diary ruin their plans. She mustn't; she *wouldn't*.

She typed two words—*Ryan Tanner*—into her favourite Internet search engine and pages of links flashed on to her screen. She knew that some of the links would be false leads, but there were sure to be one or two that related to the Ryan Tanner she'd met. With luck, she would find something she could follow up…something she could use to her advantage…to keep him quiet.

She had to find a way to stop Tanner.

He deserved this.

Didn't he?

Fifteen minutes later, she grinned at her computer screen, delighted with what she'd discovered. While it was true that Ryan Tanner was a journalist who'd worked for *The Sydney Chronicle* and a couple of London papers, it was what he had *not* told her that excited her now.

Her tormentor was actually one of the Big Name Tanners—Ryan Davidson Tanner—son and heir of the notoriously colourful and outspoken mining magnate, Jordan Davidson Tanner.

Her mind whirled with snatches of text, phrases she'd jotted down, brimming with possibilities...

distanced from the family...estranged from his father...

jealously guards his privacy...not photographed with a family member since he left school...

What couldn't she do with this?

A hot-looking single guy, heir to one of Australia's most famous business tycoons, who'd turned his back on the family fortune and chosen a life as a lowly jobbing journalist—he was a *City Girl* editor's dream come true.

And...he was a man who closely guarded his privacy.

Wow!

She'd struck gold.

But...*Oh, my gosh...*

She felt ill as her guilty conscience elbowed its way to the centre of her thoughts. If she exposed Ryan Tanner in *City Girl* against his wishes, knowing he would hate it, she was as bad as he was. This would be...

Blackmail...

Not a nice place to be.

Journalism might be a jump-down-your-throat kind of game, but Simone had always prided herself on achieving publishing success without resorting to really intrusive stories. Her magazine had integrity.

She glanced again at the sheets of information about the Tanners that she'd printed out. *Did she really want to do this?*

Under other circumstances she would never consider blackmail. But she had to stop Tanner from publishing her story, had to protect Belle and Claire on the other side of the world and she was worried sick because of the threat he posed.

She drew a deep breath.

Right. Desperate times required desperate measures. Ryan Tanner had left her no option.

He might be potentially mega-rich and undeniably good-looking…but he was also despicable and dangerous.

Toughen up, girl.

Yes! She would do this. And she would enjoy seeing Ryan Tanner exposed to the full glare of *City Girl*'s spotlight. She would enjoy letting him know that the shoe was now quite neatly on the other foot.

And why should she feel guilty? The rest of her staff would agree with her. There would be no argument. Ryan Tanner was the perfect candidate for the next instalment of *City Girl*'s hottest series, *The Secret Life of Bachelors*.

It was close to noon by the time Ryan jogged up the sun-drenched beach, dropped his surfboard on to the sand and stretched his tired, well-exercised muscles.

Flicking salty hair from his eyes, he retrieved his slim silver cellphone from deep within the folds of his beach towel.

Three missed calls—all from one source.

He frowned, debating whether he should check the caller now or later, after he'd showered and found some food. His stomach growled with hunger.

The decision, however, was made for him when the phone rang again. He answered it promptly.

"Morning." *Was it still morning?*

"Mr Tanner?"

Even though Simone Gray had dominated his thoughts for the past twenty-four hours, the unexpected sound of her voice caught him in the chest, like a surprise left hook. He had to draw two sharp, quick breaths before he could reply. "Simone."

"You're a hard man to track down," she said, injecting a note of accusation.

"I've been…uh…busy."

"Really? No one at the *Chronicle* office could tell me where you were."

"I'm not working for the *Chronicle*. I'm freelancing."

A pause. "Are you on a job at the moment?"

Ryan scratched his suntanned chest and cracked a slow smile as he looked out at the blue sea, sparkling and rolling beneath a sleepy summer sky. "More or less. I'm writing a surf report."

"You're at the beach?"

"Yeah."

He waited for her derisive *tut-tut* and was surprised when she sounded rather pleased. "Really? Which one?"

"Now why would you want to know that?" Ryan's smile tilted into a lopsided grin. "Were you thinking of donning a bikini and joining me? You should, you know. The surf's up and the sun's great. Come on down."

"In your dreams, Tanner."

"You're not a water baby?"

"I do my swimming in the Coogee rock pool *after* working hours."

An instant vision of Simone's lovely slim body leapt to life and Ryan pictured her in a swimsuit, slicing high in the water. Then he heard a soft sound, a choked-off groan, and he realised she regretted giving him that information.

But she made a quick recovery. "Tell you what," she said. "Why don't I grab one of our photographers and catch a shot of you with your surfboard?"

"Photographer?" Ryan's grin faded. "Why would you want a photographer?"

"To illustrate the great story we're running. About you, Mr Tanner. I've written it myself and I must say it's rather good. Although it's more of an exposé than our usual features."

Ryan swore beneath his breath.

Simone was playing games—which explained why she sounded so suddenly perky.

His eyes narrowed. He watched a young mother laugh as her toddler chased a seagull into the shallows and then, shifting his gaze, he watched the perfect hollow curl of a blue-green wave. "That is not a good idea," he said quietly.

"Oh, I couldn't possibly agree with you, Mr Tanner. And neither does anyone on my staff. We're all unanimous. We think this story's fabulous. Fascinating! You're the perfect subject for us."

He was aware of a clammy sensation crawling down his spine, a sensation that had nothing to do with the drying, sticky salt on his skin. "OK, I'll bite. I'm a perfect subject for exactly what kind of fabulous story?"

"For *City Girl*'s eligible bachelor archive."

Another swearword escaped him and this time it was audible. "No way!"

"In every way, Ryan. And I'm really excited about this, because we've managed to slot you in for the next edition. All we need is a really good full-colour photo. A beach shot would be fantastic."

"Forget it."

"There's no rush. If you're not feeling photogenic right now, there's still time to set something up, or we can always use one of—"

"You're crazy, Simone. This is a joke, right?"

"Mr Tanner, I'm a busy editor of a very popular magazine. I'm far too occupied with important business to waste my time writing jokes."

He couldn't help noting how different she sounded today. The defensive, frightened girl he'd met at the Jade Dragon was conducting herself with the breezy confidence he'd noted when he'd first seen her at the airport. In fact, if he wasn't mistaken, she was enjoying herself.

At his expense.

Ryan counted to five and then spoke with a deliberately casual drawl. "Simone, you're deluding yourself if you think your ambitious yuppie readers will be interested in a hack journalist-cum-beach bum."

To his horror, he realised that was almost exactly what his father would say.

"Sorry, Ryan, but that's where you're so wrong. Women, especially ambitious women, are always intrigued by rich men in disguise."

"By *what*?"

"You're a living, breathing fairy tale, you know. The Prince and the Pauper. But your cover's blown. One of my journalists is contacting your brother, Christopher, right now. We want the latest stats on the Tanner fortune."

Strike three—and he was out.

Ryan almost groaned, but knew any sound of dismay would give Simone intense satisfaction, so he released a super-soft, huffing sigh instead. She had done her homework and uncovered his family connections. It wouldn't have been too hard. No doubt she'd also found out about the bad blood between him and JD.

She would not know that Ryan had his own confidential business plan and had never touched a cent of JD's money. But he supposed that wouldn't save him from the spotlight's glare.

Her exposé was some warped kind of payback because she thought he was going to publish her diary.

This was blackmail.

"Simone, we should talk about this. We need to meet."

She didn't reply.

"Let me take you out to dinner. I owe you a meal anyway." This time he would pull out all the stops—take her to the most expensive restaurant in town, reserve the best table, order the finest wine.

Still no response.

Ryan closed his eyes and grimaced, ploughed his right hand into his hair, which had dried quickly in the sun and was stiff with salt from the sea.

"Come on, Simone. You owe me a hearing. And you owe me at least one chance to explain why you shouldn't run with this story."

"Let me sleep on it."

"*Like hell!* I want this settled now."

But his angry response was wasted. Simone had already hung up.

CHAPTER FOUR

"OH, YES! He's good!"

'Good? Is that all you can say? The man's gorgeous. Drop an "o" from that word. He's a god.'

The *City Girl* team huddled around their graphic artist's computer, staring at the breathtaking image on her screen. Simone stood to one side, three fingers pressed to her lips, watching the others' excitement with mild dismay. She wanted Ryan Tanner to make a stir, and yet...

"He's the best bachelor we've ever had," Cate breathed. "Look at those toned pecs, those abs, and that smile! Cute with a capital Q."

"Not to mention his bedroom eyes. Is he real?"

Karin, the graphic artist, laughed. "This guy's one hundred per cent authentic. Every inch real. I haven't laid a finger on him." She let out an exaggerated, dramatic sigh. "Sad to say."

Simone bit back a scoffing retort.

The image the girls were drooling over was a black and white photo of Ryan Tanner, taken a few years ago at a surfing carnival. A news photographer had taken the shot just after Ryan had finished an Iron Man Surf Lifesaving challenge, a three-part race that combined swimming, surf skis and a beach sprint.

Posed on a sunlit beach, Ryan was wearing nothing but a brief pair of black swimming trunks that left rather a lot of packaged testosterone on display. He was grinning at the camera with the easy charm that was becoming just a little too familiar for Simone's comfort.

The girls were seriously impressed.

"Think how fit he must be," Donna murmured.

Teeth gritted, Simone dragged her eyes from the screen. Having just completed her own cycling challenge, she was well aware of the training and discipline Tanner must have endured to get into shape for an Iron Man race. But she wasn't prepared to acknowledge it now, any more than she was prepared to admit that the guy was the ultimate in super-toned and suntanned masculinity.

She turned to Karin. "Do you have the name of the photographer who took this shot?"

Karin nodded. "Would you like me to contact him?"

"Might be an idea. Just in case Tanner's uncooperative and we need to run with this pic." Simone schooled her features to look bored as she flicked another glance at the screen. "Pity it's black and white. Let's see what it looks like when you zoom in a little."

With a couple of clicks of the mouse, Karin enlarged Ryan Tanner so that he filled the screen. "Too grainy," she said. "But I should be able to fix that."

Donna sighed dreamily. "Don't you love that shaggy, wet-haired, just stepped out of the shower look?"

"Adorable!" Karin stared at the screen for a moment,

then swivelled in her chair and winked at Simone. "Why don't we work on that shower concept? Drape a towel over this babe's shoulder, bare one hip. Make him look as if he's in the bathroom." Her eyes twinkled cheekily. "A bachelor for your bathroom. How's that for a fantasy? Brings him a little closer to home."

The thought of Ryan Tanner naked in her bathroom caused an unsettling tightness in Simone's chest as if every last drop of air had been squeezed from her lungs. *For heaven's sake.* She could even picture him letting the towel drop. A playful striptease. *For her eyes only...*

"That's encroaching on dangerous copyright issues," she wheezed.

Her half-choked voice brought curious glances from Donna and Cate.

"Let me have a go anyway," said Karin. "Just for us. For fun."

Without waiting for her boss's permission, she set to work, using her state-of-the-art computer wizardry to transform Ryan, while the semicircle of women watched in reverent silence. Simone tried not to look, but couldn't help it. She was fascinated.

In an amazingly short space of time, Karin had Ryan standing against a background of pale green bathroom tiles, still with his wet, sun-streaked hair, but with a baby-soft, snow-white bath towel draped over one broad, suntanned shoulder. His deeply muscled chest and taut abdomen were still on show, but now his lean right hip was bared, so that he looked as if he was wearing nothing but the towel.

A hush fell over the room. Finally Cate spoke for all

of them. "Gosh, Karin, you're a genius. This hunk will be every woman's dream."

Donna let out a soft groan. "Oh, man. He'll score a big fat tick in every box on *City Girl*'s hot-o-meter."

The girls were so intent on the image that they ignored the faint click of the door opening behind them.

"So what do you think of him now, Simone?" Karin asked.

A deeply masculine voice broke into the hushed silence. "Good question, Simone."

Simone gasped. Spun around.

Ryan Tanner. In the flesh.

In the office.

She felt her heart leap high, threatening to force its way out through her throat.

Ryan stood very tall, dominating the room, while he let his angry glare scorch each of the women gathered around the computer. Then he stared at Simone, an angry pulse beating in his jaw. His hard gaze made her insides squirm.

"So," he said coldly, "this is the way *City Girl* magazine conducts business?"

Simone winced. She was proud of her magazine. It covered serious issues close to her heart like domestic violence, abused children and street kids. But she was proud of *City Girl*'s entertainment value too and she was blowed if she was going to be feeble and defensive.

Behind Ryan in the doorway, Rosie, the front desk receptionist, was sending her a wild-eyed pantomime, finishing with a gesture of helplessness.

Simone realised in a blink what must have happened. Tanner had barged his way past poor Rosie. Ignoring the girl's protests, he'd marched right through the building until he'd found this office—*City Girl*'s inner sanctum.

"Will I call Security?" Rosie mouthed.

Simone gulped and shook her head. An angry Ryan Tanner would be more than a match for their podgy, middle-aged security guard.

She tried to glare back at him, which wasn't easy given that she was all too aware of the absurd contrast between the smiling, semi-naked fantasy on the computer screen and the scowling, fully dressed reality in the office.

Just the same, she could feel every woman in the room taking in the finer points of their intruder's tall, broad shouldered sexiness.

"Mr Tanner—" Simone's chin lifted. "This is a restricted area. Would you please wait outside?"

"No, Ms Gray, I will not." His voice hinted at the same quietly contained anger she'd sensed on the phone. "I want to speak to you."

"Then you should make an appointment."

She wished she sounded more in control, more sure of her ground—especially with her staff looking on.

Ryan offered her a mirthless smile. "We can keep this polite or I can explain to your staff exactly what you're up to." Very deliberately, he let his gaze track from her to the computer screen.

She tried not to wince.

OK, so maybe his anger was understandable. He

would be mortified if his story and this photo were published in *City Girl*. But Simone couldn't allow herself to be distracted by sympathy for a man who'd read her private diary. She still had no idea what he planned to do with that.

This was war and she had right on her side.

At least Ryan knew that she meant business now—that she would stop at nothing to protect her secret, as well as her friends'.

How wonderful to be able to say: *I've made sure he won't bother you, Belle. Nothing to worry about now, Claire. All clear. Full steam ahead.*

Ryan's gaze skewered her. "I'm sure you'll spare me the time to discuss this matter now. Otherwise—". He paused and waited a beat while her skin prickled uncomfortably.

Lifting a brave eyebrow, she said airily, "I hope you're not trying to threaten me, Mr Tanner."

To her annoyance, he smiled. "Ms Gray, this is something we need to discuss in private."

Simone was quite certain her complexion reflected every hue of a bushfire out of control. Without looking at the other girls or meeting Ryan's gaze, she spoke with all the coolness she could muster. "I could spare you five minutes in my office."

An uncomfortable silence followed. Simone could hear heavy breathing, was terrified it was coming from her.

At last Ryan said, "Five minutes with you in your office should be almost long enough."

Beside her, Donna let out a sound that was suspiciously like a choked-back giggle.

Simone shot her employee a sharp, cutting glare, then threw her shoulders back, lifted her chin and marched towards the door. "This way, Mr Tanner."

Not sparing a glance for him, or her stunned staff, she sailed out of the room, leaving Ryan to follow her down the long passage. Sweeping past her surprised PA's desk, she hurried into her own private office, where she headed straight for the safety of the high-backed leather chair behind her desk.

Ryan walked towards her and he seemed suddenly too tall and far too broad-shouldered, taking up more of her office than was surely legal. Her legs felt as limp as noodles and she sat quickly.

Ryan took his time to sit and relaxed back with his legs stretched easily in front of him, ankles crossed.

Simone swallowed. "What do you wish to discuss?"

His smile faded. "You know why I'm here, Simone. You cut me off before we finished our phone conversation."

"But we'd covered everything that mattered, hadn't we?"

He gave an impatient shake of his head. "You must realise you hit a raw nerve by threatening to link me with the Tanner fortune. I don't have anything to do with the family business. And I jealously guard my private life."

"And all that will make fascinating reading, Ryan. It's a really good story."

He looked straight at her, his gaze unnervingly direct, his eyes unexpectedly hard and challenging. "Perhaps you've underestimated my father," he said quietly. "Did you realise that if JD were displeased he'd sue? And he'd be more than happy to let the court costs mount until he put your magazine out of business."

Simone felt so suddenly dizzy she had to grip the arms of her chair. "You can't be serious. I did a little research, the way any journalist does. And I uncovered a fascinating story that would be of great interest to a lot of young women."

"Nice try, Simone, but you can't whitewash blackmail."

"Blackmail?"

"That's what this amounts to. You're terrified that I'll publish your diary, so you hunted around till you found a way to push me into a corner."

"What's sauce for the goose is sauce for the gander."

"Not this gander." He sighed. "What have I got to do to convince you that I haven't read your diary?"

This time, when Ryan's dark brown eyes looked straight into hers, there was something so honest and transparent in his gaze that Simone was forced to look away.

What if he was telling the truth?

Was that possible?

She'd been so scared, so terrified that this man knew her secret and had the power to tell it to the world. And her mind had become stuck in that groove. To suddenly trust Ryan seemed impossible, like jumping from a plane without a parachute.

Perhaps Ryan sensed her hesitation. "Come to dinner with me," he said more gently.

Simone quickly dropped her gaze. It was completely

and utterly unfair that his smile and his voice could awaken every erogenous zone in her body.

"Let me convince you," Ryan continued. "Let's talk—not as rival journalists, but as educated, civilised, ethical adults. You're very protective of your diary and rightly so. I expect you to understand that I value my privacy just as highly."

Was it really possible that they could talk this through and reach a point of understanding? Could she really put the whole sorry mess about the diary to rest?

How wonderful it would be if she could forget Ryan Tanner and get on with her real mission—finding a way to talk to her grandfather, unburdening her secret, getting his absolution.

Peace, at last.

"Where would we meet?" she asked with quiet resignation.

"That's up to you. We could try another restaurant, but last time you panicked and bolted out the door."

Did he have to remind her that this whole situation rattled her so easily?

"You should come to my place," he said. "I'll cook dinner."

Her head jerked up. "Your place?"

"Or yours."

"No." She didn't want Ryan Tanner snooping around her private domain.

"Why not my place, then?"

For a thousand reasons—and only some of them to do with the fact that she would be alone with one of the hottest bachelors in Sydney. Until now she'd always tried hard to ignore how attractive Ryan was. And she felt a little confused. Was this proposed meeting really all about settling their differences?

"This sounds like a date, Ryan."

He grinned. "Why not make it a date?"

"Because—" she gasped quickly, feeling suddenly out of her depth "—because you're jumping to conclusions."

He seemed unperturbed. "OK. It's not a date. Just a meeting. And I should warn you my place is nothing flash. But I can promise we'll be private and the dinner shouldn't be at all shabby." He sent her a charming, tummy-tumbling smile. "I can cook a mean curry."

Leaning forward, he snagged a notepad and pen from her desk and wrote down his address.

Simone watched the way his long fingers gripped the pen, admired his strong, distinctive handwriting and heard herself sigh. And she knew she was going to agree.

Ryan cast a dubious eye over the disarray of pots, chopping boards and ingredients spread about his kitchen. He'd made some smart moves in his life, but inviting Simone Gray to dinner was not one of them.

Cooking the curry wasn't the problem. It was the Simone factor…

He was getting in deep here and he wasn't absolutely certain it was a good idea. What did he want to achieve, apart from ensuring that Simone dropped his story in *City Girl*?

He remembered the way she'd looked in her office yesterday, saw again the blue fire of challenge in her lovely eyes, the haughty toss of her golden head and the proud tilt of her chin as she'd sailed out of the office. Saw the sway of her hips and the curve of her behind as he'd followed her. Her long, long legs.

Yeah, exactly…Was there really any debate about the real source of Simone Gray's irresistibility? He'd wanted her from the minute he'd set eyes on her at the airport.

He looked about his flat and knew there was little about it to impress a woman. His living space had become a kind of litmus test. If a woman didn't like the way he lived, he knew straight away that he should call it quits.

Years ago, he'd turned his back on his father's wealth. Perversely, he'd invested his inheritance from his mother in urban redevelopment schemes, but had paid little attention to how they were earning and hadn't used any of that money to finance his lifestyle. And he'd refused to tell his father about the investments. Or anyone else, actually.

He'd seen the way people sucked up to JD simply because he was mega-rich. And he'd seen the change in women, the minute they realised his family connection and his potential inheritance.

It had happened most recently in London.

After his father's interference, word about his wealthy family had spread quickly. His girlfriend at the time had been miffed that Ryan had never told her she was dating the son of one of the richest men in Australia. She'd been spitting angry for about five minutes. And then she'd become incredibly desperate—demanding and greedy and clinging. Everything had turned ugly and it had ended in a furious public row.

It was a familiar pattern. Why hadn't he learned? Why did he cling to the ideal that one day he'd find a girl who could like—*really* like—Ryan Tanner, minus JD. Someone who was willing to take him without the glamour and the fuss? It was a pipedream, no doubt. His own warped version of *Mission Impossible*.

With a grunt of frustration he lifted his knife and gave an unsuspecting carrot a rather vicious chop.

What to wear?

Simone surveyed the clothes in her wardrobe and knew she'd never felt so uncertain. She'd never been on a date camouflaged as a business meeting. Or was this the other way round?

One thing was certain—Ryan Tanner had her thoroughly confused. She wasn't sure whether she wanted to look good tonight to impress him or simply to boost her own morale.

But she knew she had to be super, super-careful this evening. She'd emailed Belle and Claire:

Tonight I hope to settle things with Ryan Tanner, once and for all, so I can set your minds at rest.

She had to keep her promise to win this final round, had to keep her wits about her. She couldn't drink too much, or talk too much, had to gain the upper hand from the outset. She most definitely mustn't allow herself to be distracted by extraneous details like Ryan's hot body or his cute, sexy smile—or his apparently excellent cooking skills.

This was still a potential spider and fly scenario. Ryan would probably try to launch some kind of charm offensive, but Simone was determined to remain immune. She had to make certain that Ryan wasn't going to publish a word about her secret—or expose anything about Belle and Claire.

It was important to hit exactly the right note tonight. Hence the big question mark hanging over her wardrobe.

She could go really casual in jeans, but that wouldn't give her the edge she needed.

Luckily she'd lost weight during the bike ride—she could squeeze back into her little black dress. It was chic. But no—it was also a cliché. And it would look as if she were trying too hard.

She considered her red skirt and jacket, but the skirt was too short and the jacket too low-cut and look-at-me. Her deep blue, pin-striped trouser suit was fine—it made her eyes bluer. But it was just a tad boring and businesslike.

Maybe white.

She reached for the sleeveless, square-necked white linen dress hanging at the back of her wardrobe, held it against her and studied her nervous reflection in the mirror. It was simply cut but stylish and it always made her feel good.

Yes, there was something about wearing white that always made her feel very safe. Probably because of all those symbolic messages about virtue and honesty. Innocence.

Oh, yes, absolutely! Wearing white was a great idea.

She wanted—no, she *needed* to ensure that Ryan Tanner kept his distance tonight.

CHAPTER FIVE

RYAN hadn't exaggerated when he'd warned Simone that his flat was nothing flash. As she stepped out of her taxi, she saw that he lived on the ground floor of an ancient terrace house, tucked away in a back street, and the general impression from the outside was of rusting gutters, crumbling bricks and peeling paint. For the son of a billionaire it was very modest indeed. Puzzling...

But when the front door opened, she was met by heavenly cooking smells. And Ryan looked good enough to eat.

He was wearing well worn and faded denim jeans, riding low over his lean hips, and an open-necked, casual white shirt. His sleeves were rolled back and revealed muscular forearms. And his suntan.

But it was his eyes that did the most damage. Beneath his sun-streaked hair, Ryan's eyes were warm brown with butterscotch highlights and they shone with intelligence and warmth. If a girl wasn't careful she could get very, very lost in them.

He smiled and said, "Wow, you look wonderful."

She was pleased, but tried not to show it, shook his

hand with exceptional formality and stepped over his threshold into a tiny vestibule decorated with an ageing spotted mirror and a crooked row of hooks.

Three more steps brought her into a large room that was Ryan's kitchen, dining and living room combined. A surfboard and a snowboard were propped in the far corner and a battered old desk held a laptop and a scattering of news clippings, copy paper, opened mail and surfing magazines. An overflowing cardboard box on the floor appeared to serve as his filing cabinet.

Well, OK, jeans might have been a better choice.

Two chairs were drawn up to a small table covered with a simple length of unhemmed blue batik cloth and the table was set with red china, crystal wineglasses and white linen napkins. In the table's centre a lighted candle sat stoutly on a terracotta saucer and the centrepiece was completed by a casual scattering of pink and white frangipani flowers.

Simone stared at the flowers, disconcerted. Ryan had gone to the trouble of setting a pretty table.

She glanced beyond the table to a line of timber-framed casement windows opened wide to welcome the thick black night and she drew a deep breath. The air was warm and fragrant with frangipani and curry spices, urging her to relax and enjoy this summer evening. But she couldn't. She mustn't. She still didn't know if she could totally trust this man.

Ryan turned to the pots simmering on the stove and she watched him adjust the heat.

"So, you weren't lying when you said you could cook curry."

He smiled and his broad shoulders lifted in a slight

shrug. "I have a limited repertoire. Hope you like lamb korma."

"If it tastes as good as it smells…" Arms folded cautiously across her chest, she took a couple of steps closer to the stove. "Actually, it smells very good. Very authentic. Did you really make this?"

His eyebrows lifted. "What kind of a question is that?"

"Well, I—"

"Are you suggesting I bought take-away and dumped it on my stove?"

"I have friends who pull that trick all the time. I've done it once or twice myself," she added as she realised she'd dented his male ego.

She offered him a smile, but quickly dropped her gaze. This man was way too distracting. Random smiles were dangerous. "We've important things to discuss, so why don't we get started?"

"In a minute. Let me get you a drink. Would you like some wine? I've rather a good white here." He opened the refrigerator door. "Or would you prefer beer?"

"Do you have a soft drink or mineral water?"

His smile turned quizzical. "You don't think something stronger will help you to relax?"

"I'm relaxed." Unfortunately, this came out just a little too snappily. "I warned you this isn't a social call, Ryan."

"Simone, chill."

She had no intention of *chilling*.

He picked up a little bowl of pistachio nuts. "Here, put these on the coffee table."

She was glad to have something to do but, as she took

the nuts, Ryan's warm fingers brushed hers and she almost dropped the bowl.

What was the matter with her?

His eyes twinkled and she wondered if he'd sensed her reaction. "Grab a seat," he said. "I'll get our drinks and join you."

Her heart was as agitated as a wild animal in a trap as she sat in a cane chair—a very deep chair piled with soft navy blue and lime striped cushions that invited her to sink back and relax. She sat well forward, knees together, ankles crossed. Sedateness incorporated.

Ryan poured a tall glass of sparkling mineral water, added ice and selected a beer for himself—a Chinese beer, she was surprised to see, and she wondered if he'd bought it especially, because of her recent trip.

He set his beer on the coffee table and handed her the mineral water and this time she was very careful to make sure that her fingers and his didn't touch.

He lowered his length into the chair opposite her, and raised his glass. "Cheers."

"Cheers."

Ryan relaxed back, with his long legs stretched under the coffee table between them. Simone sat a little straighter.

"I guess we should get started," she said, eyeing him dourly.

"First you have to promise not to run away this time. At least not before you've tasted the food."

Simone gulped. She felt embarrassed to remember the way she'd run away from the Jade Dragon. "Don't worry," she said, trying to sound offhand. "I wouldn't run away without tasting *this* food. Not after you've gone to so much trouble."

"That's good to know."

She looked up and saw Ryan's brown eyes lit by a soft glow and she sent her bones a sharp warning: *no melting.*

"By the way," he said, pointing to a bookcase made from planks of unpainted wood held in place with bricks. "That's where your diary sat for the whole time it was in my possession. It was on that shelf, gathering dust. I flipped through a few random pages, to see if I could identify the owner, but I swear I didn't read it. As a matter of fact, on the day you lost it I chased your taxi halfway across Sydney."

"Really?"

"My driver pulled out all the stops. We might have caught you if it wasn't raining."

It was some time before Simone closed her mouth. And then she nodded, prepared to admit that Ryan *might* be telling her the truth. But she felt more confused than ever.

How could she continue to think of this man as her enemy when he disarmed her at every turn?

In spite of everything, she was feeling drawn to him. And impossibly curious. Why would Jordan Tanner's son hide away in such a modest dwelling? In virtual obscurity. She had to find out more about him.

"You were going to convince me that I shouldn't feature you in *City Girl*'s bachelor series. I presume that means you'd like to tell me about your family?"

"Off the record?"

"Of course, Ryan."

He watched her thoughtfully for a moment or two and then seemed to come to a decision. "Well, I'm sure you've found out a lot about my father when you did your research, but what did you learn about my mother?"

His mother? "Nothing, actually." Simone felt a prickle of alarm. Talk of mothers almost always made her nervous.

Ryan dropped his gaze, tapped the arm of his chair with his index finger. "My mother's name was Catherine Banning."

Simone frowned, trying to remember where she'd heard that name.

"She had a short but brilliant career as an artist."

"Oh, yes, now I remember. Catherine Banning painted lovely interiors."

Ryan nodded. "And she loved music and books too. Anything in the arts, actually. Apparently I take after her as far as the books are concerned. JD and my brother have no time for books, unless they're cash books."

"So did you grow up feeling as if you were a square peg in a round hole?"

"As far as my family were concerned—always. He let out a long breath. "My mother died giving birth to me."

There was a fierce, fleeting rearrangement of his features as he tried for a grin and missed. "JD lost Catherine and got me instead. It wasn't a very fair exchange."

Simone saw the flash of raw pain in Ryan's eyes and immediately stopped worrying about herself.

"I'm sure that's not how your father felt."

"Oh, yeah. That's exactly how he felt." Ryan thumped the arm of the chair. Then he shrugged and cracked a crooked smile. "Fate made a mistake, taking away the love of JD's life and leaving me as the booby prize."

Simone gasped. "Your father told you that?"

"Not those words precisely. But the message was clear."

Ryan was pretending that he wasn't hurt. He'd probably been pretending all his life. He'd grown up feeling that he'd caused his mother's death. Simone knew only too well how truly awful that felt. But Ryan had felt alienated from his father and brother too. So lonely.

She knew that learning even one or two personal details about someone could make a huge difference to how you viewed them. But now, as she sat in Ryan's modest flat and listened to his story, the inescapable truth of that fact sank in. Suddenly it was impossible to think of Ryan as her enemy.

To her surprise, she wanted to leap out of her chair, to throw her arms around him, wanted to give him the hug his mother had never been able to give him.

Eyes stinging, she picked up her glass instead. Holding it in two hands, she said, "If *City Girl* published your bachelor story and linked it to your famous family, we'd be rubbing salt in a very raw wound, wouldn't we?"

Ryan nodded.

There was an awkward pause and Simone wondered if he would expect a similar disclosure from her.

Her panic returned. A fierce slash of fear. She tried to ignore it and took a handful of pistachio nuts from the bowl, popped one in her mouth. "If you don't mind, I don't want to talk about my family," she said, then crunched it.

"That's cool." Ryan smiled slowly. And then, after a thoughtful pause, "You still don't get it, do you, Simone? I'm not trying to find out what's in your diary. Sure, I'm curious, but I have no intention of pressing you for details. I don't plan to publish anything about you."

"I believe you," she said softly.

It was true. She did believe Ryan. Wow! It felt so good.

She hadn't realised how tense she'd been until that moment. Relief sent her sinking back into the cushions and she almost spilled her drink again. Quickly she set it back on the table.

She suppressed an urge to smile back at him. "And I assume this means you won't print anything about Belle or Claire either."

"Who are they?"

"They're girls I met on the Himalayan cycling trip."

"Oh, yeah. I think you mentioned them in the article. No, of course I won't write about them. I can't, can I? I don't have a clue."

"Well, that—that's wonderful. I'm very grateful, Ryan."

He jumped to his feet and sent her a priceless smile. "And now that's settled, it must be time to eat. Can't let the rice boil dry."

Simone nodded mutely, but she didn't move. She felt rather stunned. Ryan had brought their business to a close before they'd even eaten.

If reaching this point was so simple, why hadn't it happened yesterday in her office?

Looking about her at the table setting and the candle, smelling the wonderful aromas from the kitchen, she knew the answer.

This was, most definitely, not a business meeting.

From the stove, Ryan called, "Could you give me a hand to put things on the table?"

She looked at the table, smelled the fragrant curry, saw Ryan in the kitchen—all broad shoulders and suntan and sexy jeans.

Oh, man, Simone. Do you really know what you're getting into here?

Suddenly it didn't seem to matter. Taking a deep breath, she stood and crossed to the kitchen.

Ryan was draining the steaming rice and she saw that it was fluffy and perfect—a result she fluked on very rare occasions.

"If you put this rice on the table," he said, "I'll bring the rest."

"Sure."

This time she forgot to keep her fingers out of the way as he handed her the bowl and the warmth of his skin sent a flash of fire zinging up her arm. Her susceptibility to this man was alarming.

Ryan became remarkably efficient, transferring the curry into an earthenware serving bowl, retrieving poppadams from the oven where they'd been keeping warm, and a cucumber and rocket salad from the fridge. Then he held up a bottle of wine.

"You'll have a little of this with your meal, won't you?"

Her eyes widened as she glanced at the label. It was an excellent vintage.

"Thank you."

He flicked off the kitchen light. "So we can't see the cooking mess." He gave her another of his lethal smiles.

The room became a different place, almost a cave, lit only by the flickering candle on the table and a lamp in the far corner. They took their seats and the frangipani and the meal smelled exotic and alluring.

Anyone looking in from the outside would think that Ryan was trying to seduce her.

Her insides tumbled at the thought.

She said little as he poured her wine and they helped themselves to the food. She took her first mouthful. And then another and another.

"Mmm...oh, wow! This is sensational, Ryan."

Across the table, their eyes met.

"The curry's not too hot for you?"

Perhaps it was a trick of the candlelight, but something in the way he looked at her made her tremble.

She dropped her gaze and, when she looked up again, Ryan was still watching her. He smiled and she almost melted off her chair and on to the floor.

"No, it's not too hot," she said. "Honestly, I like it spicy. This is just how I love it. It's perfect."

She was sure her face was bright red. The air between them quivered with innuendo, as if they had not been talking about the food at all, but something else entirely.

Sex...

Some like it hot...

Simone took a swift drink of cold wine and told herself she was imagining things.

But was she?

Was she?

For so long she'd managed to deny the thread of attraction that had linked her to Ryan from that first moment they'd locked eyes at the airport. But now, alone with him in his house and sharing this lovely meal, it was impossible to ignore the chemistry.

Her heart went crazy again, fluttering like a giddy fool.

When she glanced up, Ryan was still looking at her.

"You're so beautiful," he said softly.

She couldn't breathe.

It was not the first time a man had told her this, but too often in the past it had sounded like the world's worst pick-up line. Ryan's eyes and his voice made the words sound genuine. Her insides tightened and coiled.

Help. It was all happening. Ryan was charming her senseless and she was allowing herself to be totally, totally drawn under his spell.

In the candlelight his lips had a very masculine, almost sculptural beauty and she couldn't help wondering how they would feel, how they would taste.

She forked rice and curry on to the edge of a poppadam, bit into it and smiled. "This is so-o-o good."

They were both a little lost for words as they continued eating and she tried to think of something to say, something light—but she'd spent so much of her life fighting shadowy fears that she'd never developed the habit of banter and small talk.

Ryan's surfboard in the corner caught her eye. "Do you spend a lot of time at the beach?" she asked.

He grinned. "More than I probably should."

"It keeps you fit." She couldn't resist casting an approving eye over his broad shoulders and the stretch of his shirt across his chest. "What do you love most about surfing?"

He thought about it. "The fact that you rely on nothing more than your own skill on a board and your understanding of the sea."

"Man against the elements?"

"More like man in harmony with the elements. But no matter how good you think you are, your success or failure is ultimately in the hands of nature."

"And you prefer surfing to team sports," she suggested.

"Much to my father's disgust." He frowned as if he hadn't meant to add that last comment.

"I'm something of a lone wolf too. I like swimming and cycling, but I prefer to compete against my own personal best rather than against others."

"What about the Himalayan cycling challenge?" Ryan helped himself to another poppadam. "That was a team effort, wasn't it?"

"Yes, but we only became a team during the journey. None of us had ever met before we started." She took a sip from her glass, set it down carefully and fiddled with its stem. "It was quite amazing really. I never expected to make such close friends as Belle and Claire in such a short space of time."

She helped herself to some extra curry. But when that

was finished and Ryan offered more she patted her very satisfied stomach. "I've eaten more than I should."

"I hope you've left room for dessert." His eyes twinkled at her.

"There's dessert as well? Ryan, I'm seriously impressed."

"Wait till you see it before you get too excited."

She jumped to her feet. "Let me help you to clear the table."

"Just pile everything next to the sink."

"Shall I fetch dishes and spoons?"

"No need." Ryan opened his freezer and held up a commercial ice cream in a paper packet and offered her a gorgeous naughty-boy smile. "Confession time. I *did* buy these."

Setting her hands on her hips, she playfully reproached him. "Not good enough, Mr Tanner."

"But at least I'm being up front about it," he said as he unwrapped a dainty chocolate-coated heart on a stick. "You must appreciate my honesty."

"I appreciate anyone who offers me chocolate and ice cream."

His eyes danced and he took a step closer. Simone wished he hadn't. Now, without the table separating them, she felt vulnerable, exposed to his potent masculinity.

He handed her the chocolate heart.

"Aren't you having one?"

"In a minute."

Their gazes locked as she took a bite.

She tried to think of something light-hearted to say,

could think of nothing, so bit into her ice cream again. She was sure it would be wise to return to the table, but she didn't. She remained there in the middle of Ryan's kitchen, spellbound, while he watched her eat her ice cream, while heat and desire circled her like a lasso.

"You have chocolate on your lip," he murmured huskily.

He was so close now that all it would take was a dip of his head and they would be kissing close. Simone hardly dared to breathe as she took the last bite, as he took the ice cream stick from her fingers and tossed it into the sink behind him.

Then, before she could come to her senses, Ryan's hands cupped her face and their eyes locked. "I've wanted to kiss you ever since I first saw you at the airport."

She tried to remember why this was crazy, but she couldn't keep her mind on the task. With Ryan's sexy mouth mere inches from hers, there was only one possible response.

She lifted her face to his.

Fine tremors rippled over and under her skin as his arms came around her, as his hips settled against her, and his mouth claimed hers.

Her lips were cool from the ice cream, but they quickly warmed beneath his heat. He kissed her gently, confidently, without haste, but with excruciating thoroughness.

Oh, my. Talk about chemistry.

Within seconds, she was helpless, lost in the masculine power of this man, in the magic of his warm, potent mouth possessing hers, his strong arms about her, his gorgeous body hard against her.

Seduction at its sweetest, at its most compelling. She wanted to melt into him, lose herself in him.

Her breasts pressed into his chest, her stomach met his hardness, and she felt a jolt of longing so fierce and hot and sweet that a moan broke from her.

She heard a choked answering groan from him and his lips were hot and hard on her throat. Her desire spiralled and she wriggled closer, angling to satisfy the alarming need in her.

A thunderous knocking sounded on the front door.

Simone jumped.

Ryan broke away, breathing hard, cursed softly and glared in the direction of the door. "I've no idea who that can be."

The knocking sounded again, even louder if possible.

"I don't believe this." He sighed heavily, pressed a kiss to her forehead. "Excuse me, Simone."

Dazed and breathless, Simone sank against a cupboard. She heard the door open and Ryan's shocked, "What are you doing here?"

"If you'd return my calls this wouldn't be necessary."

She could hear every word, clear as a bell. The caller was a man—an older man—and he sounded angry. She tried to tidy her hair.

"Why the hell is this place in darkness?" the caller growled. "Haven't you paid your electricity bills, Ryan? Have they cut off your power?"

Good grief. Who was this?

"I have company," Ryan replied, sounding weary,

almost as if he was used to this kind of exchange. "I don't have time for another of your lectures and my guest isn't interested in anything we have to say to each other."

"I don't care if you're entertaining the head of the World Bank or a high-class hooker. I want to talk to you, son."

Son? This was Ryan's father, the infamous JD Tanner? Simone looked about her, wondering if she should make a dash for the bathroom.

"You should have warned me you were coming," Ryan said.

"If you'd return my calls I wouldn't have to spend time and money trying to get a few words with you."

"So that's what's eating you. The cost of a plane ticket to find me. Send me the bill, why don't you?"

"Don't be so damn touchy, Ryan. I've got a great opportunity for you, and for once in your life you need to listen to me."

"I told you I have a guest."

Simone felt terrible to be eavesdropping on this exchange. Again, she wondered if she should try to make herself scarce. But heavy footsteps sounded and suddenly a thickset man with beetling brows appeared from behind the strip of wall that screened the front door and she recognised the face she'd seen so often in the media.

JD Tanner took in the scene in a flash—the darkened room, the table set for two, the flickering candlelight. His eyes narrowed shrewdly when he saw Simone. Behind him, Ryan looked ready to commit homicide.

Making a hasty decision, Simone stepped forward and offered Ryan's father her hand, remembering only when it was too late that it was probably sticky from the ice cream. "Good evening, Mr Tanner, I'm Simone Gray."

JD blinked and quickly dredged up his social skills. "Delighted to meet you, Simone." He let his gaze rake over her. "Well, well, obviously you work for the World Bank."

It was a quick yet subtle apology for his tasteless suggestion that she might be a hooker and Simone almost smiled, but she took her cue from Ryan, whose face remained as serious as a heart attack.

"Ms Gray and I are discussing a business matter, Dad."

It was the first time during their exchange that Ryan had addressed his father as 'Dad' and Simone noted a tense, wary look pass between the two men.

"We have unfinished business," Ryan continued more equably. "You're a businessman, so you must understand that we need to be left alone. I'll call you tomorrow. I promise."

JD nodded but his sharp eyes continued to study Simone. She hoped he couldn't see that her lips were puffy and tender from his son's kisses.

"What business are you in, Simone?"

"I'm a journalist." Lifting her chin to meet his authoritative stare, she almost called him sir, but resisted the temptation.

He let out an impatient grunt. "Another scribbler. I should have known."

"Simone's the editor of *City Girl* magazine," Ryan interposed.

"Editor?"

"Executive editor," added Ryan.

JD let his glittering gaze settle on her again and she felt like a hapless bug, squirming beneath an entomologist's spyglass.

She wondered if her hair was very mussed, if she had a smear of chocolate on her cheek. For all sorts of reasons, she was grateful that she'd chosen to wear the white dress tonight.

JD's frown didn't soften, but she fancied she caught a sparkle, a glimmer of something like approval in his eyes.

"Well…I dare say you two have a great deal of business to complete," he said at last. For a beat or two he stood, watching them both, then he cast a critical glance over the flat before he slapped his hands against his thighs. "All right. I'll leave my business till tomorrow."

He favoured Simone with a charming smile that transformed his face and, for the first time, she saw a family resemblance between father and son.

Then, as abruptly as he'd come, JD wished them a curt goodnight, turned suddenly and left the room.

From the front doorway he called a final parting barb. "If you get the chance, Simone, try to talk some business sense into that stubborn blockhead son of mine."

Ryan let out an angry sigh, stood with his shoulders hunched and his hands sunk deep in the pockets of his jeans. His father, with his impeccable sense of timing, had ruined everything. Again.

He shot a wary glance in Simone's direction and she sent him a tentative smile. "So that's what a mining magnate looks like at close range."

Ryan rolled his eyes. "JD wouldn't recognise a mine if he fell down a shaft."

"You're joking." Her blue eyes expressed clear disbelief. "But he owns so many mines. Practically everyone in Australia has heard of your father. His involvement in mining is huge."

Ryan's lip curled into a sneer. "Oh, yes, my father's made a big name for himself—because he's made plenty of money. He didn't start off as a prospector or a miner, but he knows how to line his pockets with the mines' profits."

Her eyebrows rose.

Ryan gave a weary shake of his head. He knew he sounded bitter and twisted, but JD always got him so stirred he couldn't think straight.

It annoyed the hell out of him. After all these years, he still couldn't control his emotions when he came face to face with his old man. JD always walked away with an emotional victory, leaving Ryan to feel as if he'd taken a kicking on a bar room floor.

"I'm especially glad we're killing the bachelor story now," Simone said.

"You can see why I've broken out of the bloody Tanner mould."

She turned and picked up some plates and set them in the sink, as if she planned to tidy up the kitchen.

"Leave that."

"It's OK." She turned on a tap. "I must say your father has a certain underlying charm."

"Leave it," Ryan barked, grabbing her wrist.

She froze.

Ryan dropped his hand. Sighed again. Everything about the night felt wrong now. It was the story of his life. Over and over, whenever he was on to a good thing—something really important—JD turned up, or did his best to interfere from long range. The fiasco in London was a prime example. And now, Ryan hadn't been back a month and it was happening again. In front of Simone.

His fists clenched. Heaven help him, one of these days he might really lose control and land a punch on the old man.

"I should probably go," Simone said.

He sighed, felt hollow inside. She shot him a look and crossed to the coffee table where she'd left her purse.

"You don't have to go." Ryan walked towards her, smiled his most appealing smile. "Don't go."

She gave a sad little shrug and he knew the evening's mood had been completely destroyed. Simone was probably regretting their incredible kiss.

Without another glance at him, she whipped out her mobile phone and began punching digits.

"If you must go, let me drive you."

She paused and looked at him, frowning.

"Come on," he urged. "I only had that one beer before dinner." Driving her home was the least he could do, given that a lovely evening had fallen to pieces. Thanks to his old man. "Please don't run off again on my account." He smiled and was pleased to see her frown disappear. "We were getting on famously before my family got in the road."

CHAPTER SIX

RYAN seemed to thaw on the journey home.

Simone was relieved. He'd been completely rocked by his father's intrusion and she'd found it unnerving. She'd had enough family problems in her past without getting involved in someone else's.

It was quite bizarre the way their roles had reversed. When she'd set out this evening, she'd been the one who was tense—and yet she'd progressed, during the course of one meal, from deep suspicion to complete trust. So many things she'd learned about Ryan. So many wrong impressions unlearned.

Such a lovely, lovely, sensational kiss.

And then his father had barged in and it was almost as if he'd pulled a switch. The beautiful evening had fallen apart. Ryan had fallen apart, his vulnerability exposed.

Simone had recognised his pain, had understood too well. And she was relieved, as they drove through the dark Sydney streets, that Ryan was slowly coming back to life. He entertained her with easy chatter about a funny movie he'd seen last week and by the time they reached the end of her street they were both laughing.

"That's my building over there," she said, pointing to the tall block of modern apartments halfway down the street. "There's a parking space opposite."

She wondered if she should invite Ryan in for coffee. Would he read too much into that? Their kiss had been off the scale, but it wouldn't be wise to take things any further. *It wouldn't, would it?*

"Thanks very much," she said. "I'm glad we had the chance to talk everything through. And the meal was wonderful."

"My pleasure."

Was this goodbye? She wondered if she would ever see him again and was rather startled by the unhappy pang in her heart at the thought of Ryan Tanner disappearing from her life.

"What about coffee?"

Goodness. The words had spilled out before she had time for second thoughts.

"Except I—I usually have hot chocolate at this time of night," she added awkwardly.

Oh, no. Was that worse? Now she sounded like a nervous schoolgirl.

But Ryan didn't seem to notice. "You've tempted me," he said and there was a definite smile in his voice. "I don't think I've had hot chocolate since I was at boarding school."

"Right."

She was super-conscious of his tall, very masculine presence beside her as they crossed the dark road and climbed the dimly lit stairs to her apartment. She tried to think about hot chocolate and conversation, but kept remembering his kiss. Her skin felt warm and tight all over.

It was almost a relief to be inside her apartment. To switch on the lights. *Home ground.*

The layout of her living area and kitchen was open-plan, much like Ryan's flat, but her apartment was much bigger. Very shiny and new, of course, and she'd splashed out on expensive, trendy furnishings.

Heading straight for the kitchen, she filled a saucepan with milk and set it on the stove. "Grab one of those stools while I make this. Or are you sure you wouldn't prefer coffee?"

"Hot chocolate's fine."

Ryan looked about the apartment, taking in her purple feature wall and the mezzanine-level study, the minimalist storage unit and wide expanse of blonde timber flooring. "This is very nice."

"Thanks. I suppose you were expecting something more traditional and suburban."

"Not especially. Why should I?"

He was looking at her blankly.

He hadn't a clue.

Simone almost skipped with delight. If she'd wanted final proof that Ryan had not read her diary, here it was. She'd written at length about a fantasy from her childhood—her dream of a four-bedroom brick home, surrounded by pergolas and gardens, with a jacaranda tree in the front yard. She'd described every room in detail...the island bench in the kitchen, the sunken lounge...a dining room big enough for Christmas and birthday parties.

Ryan was looking puzzled and she turned quickly and buried her face in a cupboard and made a business of selecting mugs. "Part of me has always wanted a very traditional suburban home," she told him over her shoulder. "A sop to my deepest insecurities, I should think."

"Oh, I don't know. It sounds very—"

"Unimaginative?" She spun around, clutching the mugs to her chest, her favourite mugs with blue-green dragonflies painted on them.

His smile was reproachful. "Unimaginative was not the word I had in mind. As a matter of fact, I can understand. I was envious of kids in the suburbs when I was growing up. I lived in a huge mansion, but all I wanted was a butter-box house with a backyard barbecue, a basketball hoop and a clothes-line full of washing."

"And kids next door to play street cricket," Simone said, smiling.

"You've got the picture." Ryan's smile was so warm Simone had to turn away quickly and concentrate very hard on spooning chocolate into mugs.

It was time to remember the lecture she'd given herself at the start of this evening. No melting over Ryan Tanner. Time to remember that nothing had really changed for her. She was still an emotional mess inside. Still had a trail of broken relationships behind her...

Like the house with the jacaranda tree in the suburbs, a lasting love was a fantasy for her, a silly pipedream. Her burdensome secret got in the way of her happiness. Every time.

Behind her the saucepan of milk threatened to boil over and she turned to lift it from the heat.

"There's a light blinking on your phone. Probably a voice message," Ryan said as she poured hot milk into mugs.

The telephone was sitting on the counter and she gave it a cursory glance as she stirred briskly to dissolve recalcitrant blobs of powdered chocolate. Belle or Claire might have called, anxious to know if she'd struck a deal with Ryan. Or perhaps they had news of their own.

"Excuse me," she said and she quickly dialled her message bank. It wasn't Belle or Claire.

It was her grandfather's housekeeper.

As soon as Simone heard her voice, she felt a betraying lump in her throat.

"Simone, it's Connie Price here. I thought I ought to warn you that I've been trying to persuade Jonathan to make contact with you, but he flatly refuses. He's become very stubborn and hard-hearted of late, but there it is. I'm sorry, dear. There's not much more I can do. Coming up to Christmas, I thought you should know how the land lies."

Connie's message felt like stones pelting Simone. She dropped the receiver and sank on to the stool in dismay. If her grandfather refused to talk to her, how could she ever make her dreadful confession? Gain his absolution?

"Not bad news, I hope."

The worst.

She looked up to find Ryan watching her, his dark

eyes so sympathetic and gorgeous that her heart did a tumble-turn. "A message about my grandfather," she said, swiping at the corner of her eye. "He's not ill or anything. It's just I—I haven't heard from him for ages."

"Does he live in Sydney?"

"Out west, on a sheep station called Murrawinni. On the other side of the Warrumbungle Ranges." She set the teaspoon she'd been using to stir their drinks in the sink. Took a deep breath. "I used to live out there when I was young and I had such a good time. I loved it."

Ryan's eyes widened with such obvious interest that she decided to be brave and to tell him more.

"My father was a soldier in Vietnam and he died before I was born, so my mother took me to live with my grandfather. I spent my early childhood running free with the bush children and learning to ride horses."

She handed Ryan his mug of chocolate.

"Sounds like fun."

"It was wonderful. There was an endless stream of pet lambs—orphans I fed bottles of milk and fell deeply in love with. And Grandfather used to take me in his canoe to catch fish. And he'd fry them over a campfire on the riverbank."

"Lucky you."

But the luck hadn't lasted.

Simone had learned very early that happiness never lasted. When she was ten, her mother had married again and they'd gone back to Sydney to live with Harold Pearson, her new stepfather. And life had never been the same.

"Come and find a more comfortable seat over here on a sofa," she said, not wanting to think about the horrors of her mother's second marriage.

They crossed the room to the matching black wool sofas and Simone wondered if Ryan was going to sit next to her, but after a slight hesitation he chose the sofa opposite, with the coffee table between them.

"Tell me more about your grandfather," he said once he was settled.

To her dismay, she discovered that she couldn't go on. The memory of Harold Pearson silenced her, bringing with it a sudden, all too familiar, rush of dread.

Damn. She'd been doing so well telling Ryan about her grandfather. If only she could talk about her family the way any girl might.

But other girls didn't have mothers who'd died in jail after killing their husbands. Other girls didn't have her dreadful memories. Her terrible secret.

She sipped at her drink and then forced a smile. "That's enough about me. Tell me what you're going to write about now that you're freelancing. Any stories about surfing?"

"Oh…one or two." He looked down at his drink, as if he was considering what to tell her. "There's a big story that I'm really keen to pull off about the sportswear and leisure companies that uncover hidden hotspots in places like French Polynesia and Java. They move in and make a packet, while the locals miss out. I'd like to see the local people get more benefits from sharing their beaches with the kings of commerce."

Simone swallowed her surprise. Somehow, she'd expected something less serious from Ryan—coverage of surfing competitions, perhaps.

"Good for you," she said warmly. "It's important to publish stories that stick up for the underdog, isn't it? What else?"

"Well, there's the search for the ultimate wave. There's a phenomenon in the Southern Ocean down off Tasmania called a sea mount. It's possibly the home of the biggest wave in the world. I'd give my eye-teeth to cover that." He shot her a puzzled quarter-smile. "But you don't really want a blow-by-blow breakdown of my work, do you?"

If she was honest, she would have to admit that she was becoming more and more interested in everything about Ryan. The fact that they shared the same profession was an added bonus. And talking about work was safer than talking about families.

Ryan drained his mug, studied the dragonfly painted on its side, then set it down on the coffee table. "I'm sorry I let my father rattle me tonight. I spoiled our evening," he said.

"You made a good recovery."

His eyes held hers. "I was hoping we could go on seeing each other."

Simone's heart seemed to shift from its usual position in her chest.

This was the crunch.

She really liked Ryan, but how could she be the right woman for him? She was hopeless at relationships. Always held back the deepest part of herself, for fear that she'd spill her secret.

The only guys she could safely date were fellows who didn't get too serious. And she was beginning to suspect that, despite his surfer boy sexiness, Ryan was the deep and meaningful type. She always dodged that—deeper emotional involvement. Apart from the extraordinary outpouring to Belle and Claire in the Himalayas, her golden rule was to avoid any situation where she might be expected to talk about her past, her family. Her secret.

Hence her string of broken relationships.

Ryan was watching her intently, waiting for an answer.

She took a deep breath and released it slowly. "This might sound strange when we've only just met, but as you've probably worked out from the way I carried on about my diary, I have a few issues." She set her mug down. "I know you have difficulties with your father, but I've made an art form out of not talking about my family."

She looked down at her hands twisting in her lap. "There's stuff I don't want to have to tell anyone, so I get nervous when things get deep or personal. I always try to hold back on my emotions and eventually…well…it doesn't bode very well for my relationships."

She looked up, expecting to see Ryan's disapproval and was shocked by the tender compassion in his dark brown eyes. But then his mouth tilted in a wry smile. "So you see yourself as something of a challenge?"

"Oh, I'm a definite challenge, Ryan. And who needs that?"

"Damned if I know." His eyebrows lifted. "As far as

I can see, these things never make sense. There's very little logic in the laws of attraction."

Attraction.

Wow!

He'd as good as acknowledged the connection she'd sensed from the first moment they'd seen each other. Simone's heart began a drum roll. She ran her tongue over dry lips.

"But let's not jump the gun here," he said. "I'm not suggesting we have to sign up for a lifelong gig." His gaze held hers and he smiled again. "That doesn't mean we shouldn't enjoy getting to know each other."

He was right, wasn't he? She was crazy to be tying herself in knots over her inability to have a long-term relationship, when all she and Ryan had shared was one meal, a cup of chocolate and one kiss. One earth-shattering kiss, admittedly.

She smiled nervously.

"So what do you think?" he said.

Her heart pounded strangely. She didn't think she'd ever been so attracted to any man.

Ryan got to his feet. "I'm happy to take this one step at a time. If you're interested, that is."

Oh, yes, she was interested. "One step at a time sounds fine."

She stood too and Ryan reached for her hands and drew her towards him, threading his fingers through hers and locking them lightly by her sides.

Simone tensed with excitement, anticipating another scrumptious kiss, but Ryan touched his lips to her forehead in a kiss so gentle that she could hardly feel it. He kissed each eyelid with feather-light brushes.

It was the most thrilling, maddening sensation. Her skin became the focus of her concentration as Ryan's lips lighted on her cheeks, her chin, her throat. Each touch was exquisitely soft, but with just enough pressure to be drop-dead sexy. She strained to savour every delicate caress.

He kissed her throat, paying it such deliberate and tender attention she thought she might swoon.

When would he reach her lips? She was almost jumping out of her skin with waiting for the prize of Ryan's lips on hers.

But suddenly, without warning, Ryan stepped away. *No!*

The look on her face must have shown him how surprised she was.

"We're taking this slowly. Remember?" He smiled and touched her once, very lightly, on the tip of her nose, then turned and began to walk across the living room, heading for the front door. "Thanks for the chocolate," he called over his shoulder.

And then, "Would you like to go out somewhere tomorrow night?"

Tomorrow night? It took a moment or two for her brain to catch up with the sudden turn of events. "Thank you," she said at last. "I'd like that."

"I'll call you tomorrow, then."

Breathless, Simone sank to the sofa. What had Ryan done to her? She had never been so aroused, and he hadn't even kissed her lips. *How* had he done it?

* * *

The light was blinking on Ryan's phone when he got home. He scowled at it, tossing up whether he really needed to check messages at this time of night. It might be another annoying tirade from his father. Then again, it could be about a job...

He pressed the button.

"Ryan, it's Simone. I'm sorry. I've just remembered I'm not free tomorrow evening. I have this weekly commitment. I don't know how I forgot, but it completely slipped my mind. I thought I'd better let you know straight away—save you making plans and having to cancel. Maybe another time?"

A heavy sigh escaped him. What was this about? The first of Simone's avoidance tactics?

He pressed his fingers against his closed lids and couldn't believe how disappointed he felt. If he wasn't careful he could make a fool of himself over this girl. Maybe he already had.

Jaw clenched, he picked up the phone. If she offered some lame excuse for cancelling their date, he would have no more to do with her. There was a limit.

He dialled her number. "Simone," he said abruptly the minute she answered.

"Is that you, Ryan?" She sounded sleepy and he pictured her in bed in something pale and silky.

His heart thudded heavily. "I—I just got your message."

"I'm really sorry I can't make it tomorrow night."

"So you said." His face twisted in a grimace. Flopping into a lounge chair, he drew a steadying breath before he spoke again. "I guess this is a busy time of the year. So many pre-Christmas parties."

"It's not a Christmas party, Ryan. I would have invited you to come with me if it was something straightforward. I'm sorry, I should have remembered about tomorrow night." She hesitated and then said, "I wasn't thinking too clearly when you left."

Ryan supposed she had a point. They'd both been a tad distracted.

"I—I teach swimming on Wednesday nights."

"Swimming?" It was the last thing he'd expected.

"Yes—to street kids."

Street kids! Momentarily, Ryan was shocked into silence. His brain had been churning up possibilities. Simone attended a yoga class on Wednesday nights, or an art class, had her legs waxed—but swimming lessons for street kids! That one had slipped right under the radar!

But perhaps he shouldn't be so surprised. Her bike ride through the Himalayas had raised money for street kids. No doubt this was another clue to the real Simone, the woman below the surface, the woman he wanted to discover.

"Well, that's fine. It's a great idea," he said, trying for a balance between sounding interested but not too nosy. "I bet the kids love their lessons."

"They do." She sounded relieved, happy that he approved. "It's a fairly low-key thing, but you'd be surprised how seriously they take their swimming. There are just three of them and they have fun, of course, but it's more than just fun. They really put an effort into practising their breathing and their strokes. Swimming gives them confidence, helps their self-image, I guess. And it's another important life skill, of course."

"I think it's a fantastic thing to do, Simone." Leaning back in the chair, he grinned at the ceiling, absurdly happy.

"Afterwards we usually go to a hamburger joint. Actually…" She hesitated.

"Yes?"

"This probably sounds crazy, Ryan."

"Try me."

"Feel free to say no, but I wondered if you'd like to join us. For hamburgers."

Without hesitation he said, "I would. I'd like that. Very much."

"A friend of mine is going to join us tonight," Simone warned Homer, David and Pink the next evening as they walked from the Coogee rock pool to the nearest hamburger joint.

Twelve-year-old David scowled at her suspiciously. "Who is he?"

"A really nice guy. His name's Ryan."

"Is he your boyfriend?" asked Pink, a shy, too thin girl of thirteen.

Simone was about to say no. How could she presume so much? But these three would mistrust a stranger. "Yes, he's my boyfriend. And I'm very keen on him, so I don't want you guys to stuff this up for me."

Pink smirked, David rolled his eyes and grinned, but Homer hung back, hands plunged in pockets, and kicked at an empty can, sending it spinning into the gutter. "Maybe I won't bother with hamburgers tonight," he said. "I'm not hungry."

Simone knew this wasn't true. Homer was always ravenous. But he wasn't prepared to trust a stranger.

"Tell you what," she said, remembering Ryan's enthusiasm last night when she'd told him about her involvement with these kids. "I reckon, if you play your cards right, Ryan would teach you how to ride his surfboard."

"I already know how to ride a board," scoffed the boy, but they all knew this was a bald-faced lie. Homer was the weakest swimmer of the three.

"Would he teach me?" David's brown eyes shone up at Simone from beneath dark, tangled curls, still damp from swimming. He was fifteen months younger than Homer and the rivalry between the two was fierce.

"I'll ask him. He's a top competitor. You'd be lucky, David." Out of the corner of her eye she saw Homer's face tighten.

They were close to the café now and Ryan was waiting outside, standing beneath a neon sign that sent red and blue flickers over his T-shirt.

"Is that him?" breathed Pink, running her fingers through her spiky red hair, trying to finger comb it into submission. "Wow, Simone, he looks like a dude."

Coming from tough little Pink, this was high praise indeed.

Simone cast a quick glance over her shoulder. Homer was only a short distance behind them. She sent the boy an encouraging smile, knowing how much he wanted to stay and understanding his wariness and fear of the unknown. Homer lived by his wits and not all his activities were legal, so he had to be eternally cautious.

"I asked Ryan to come tonight because I wanted him to meet you," she said. "But if you really don't want him here, Homer, he'll understand."

The boy stood, staring at the footpath, then he sighed and shot a narrow eyed glance towards Ryan. "You swear he's OK?"

"I swear."

"S'pose it won't hurt," he muttered.

That settled, and feeling rather like a mother hen with her chicks, she took her gang of three to meet her newly promoted boyfriend.

"So where are they off to now?" Ryan asked at the end of the meal as they watched the trio head away from the beach and into the night.

He'd been a great success with the children. Pink appeared to be smitten the minute she'd set eyes on him and had become rather tongue-tied and coy, but both David and Homer had thawed in the warmth of Ryan's relaxed friendliness.

David, a very keen swimmer now, had asked lots of questions about surfing. Homer, more practical, had sussed out the chances of earning money waxing surfboards.

"We don't want to know where they're going," Simone said softly. "Pink sometimes goes home, if she thinks it's safe. She's what's known as a child *on* the streets rather than a child *of* the streets. She comes and goes, but the boys—" She shook her head. "They don't tell me and I know they don't want me to ask."

Turning to Ryan, she saw pain and compassion in his

face and she had to fight an impulse to kiss him, there on the footpath, under the street light.

"There's a point where I have to draw the line," she said. "I teach them swimming. At the moment that's all I can do."

"How did you meet them?"

"I wrote a story about street kids. I interviewed a lot of the people who helped them and I became more and more interested. I started working in one of the kitchens, just once a week, but then I heard about a new sports programme they were introducing. Some kids were getting into team sports, but there were others, like my little crew, who didn't mix well."

She sent him a twinkling smile. "Lone wolves, like us. And, well, I was a swimmer—" She shrugged again. "We took it from there."

"And what are *we* going to do now?" he asked, taking her hand.

His skin was warm, his hand strong and his touch sent a delicious tingle through her, down her arms and back, all the way to her toes.

"I think *I* should head home," Simone said. Straight home. Alone. To a cup of hot chocolate and a good book.

But Ryan had other ideas. "Why don't we take a walk on the beach? We can sit on the sand and listen to the sea." He grinned at her. "Come on, you'll love it. It's one of my favourite things to do."

Getting to know Ryan better was one thing, but a walk on the beach sounded too romantic. *Dangerously* romantic. Simone struggled with her conscience for a full two seconds before she gave in. After all, how could she say no? Ryan had been so sweet with her little trio.

The sand still retained some of the day's warmth and a fresh salty breeze blew in from the water. They sat in companionable silence, staring at the almost full moon which lit up the beach and made a silver path across the inky-black water from the horizon to the breaking surf.

Ryan was content to listen while Simone told him more about the children—about Pink's unstable home life, David's detox programme, and how Homer, who had taken to the streets after his single mother died of a drug overdose, earned a little money by collecting shopping trolleys for supermarkets.

Leaning back on his elbows, Ryan watched Simone's lovely face in the moonlight. "These kids have real problems. It kind of puts my complaints about JD into perspective."

She nodded. "Street kids are so gutsy. When you think of the abuse and the pain they've been through, it's a miracle they get up and face the world on a daily basis."

"You're passionate about them, aren't you?"

In the moonlight her eyes lost their sparkle. "There was a time when I came within a hair's breadth of being a street kid myself."

"You mean you almost ran away from home?"

She nodded again. "My stepfather was very—" Her mouth tightened and she turned her head so he couldn't see her face. "He had a drink problem and he used to beat my mother."

Metres away, waves dumped heavily on to the shore. A chill crept down Ryan's spine. He was almost certain that this stepfather was at the heart of Simone's troubles, part of the dark secret she'd alluded to.

She drew nervous lines in the sand with her finger. "But I can't talk about it." She looked up at him and he saw the silver shimmer of tears. Her mouth pulled out of shape and she jumped to her feet, hurried away from him, over the sand.

Unsure whether he should follow her, Ryan waited and, before long, she stopped and turned, looking back at him.

She looked beautiful as she stood there, hair shining in the moonlight. Even more beautiful as she began to walk back to him, her hips swaying rhythmically as she came across the silver sand, slowly, purposefully, her eyes locked with his. His body tightened as she knelt on the sand at his side.

If only he had the power to free her from the crushing burden of her past. Something very dark must have happened. He felt certain that she longed to be able to talk about it. Get it out in the open and have done with it.

"I'm sorry, Ryan," she said. "But I did warn you about my hang-ups."

He touched her arm very lightly with his fingertips. Her skin was warm and smooth and soft. Infinitely touchable. "You don't have to tell me anything you don't want to."

Time seemed to stand still. Ryan was aware of the beat of his blood and the faint hum of Coogee traffic behind him. Looking up, he could see the glossy sheen of stars, could hear the crash and thump of the surf. Saw

Simone, her hair moon-silver, looking like a mermaid temptress as she knelt beside him.

They were supposed to be taking this slowly, but his feelings for her were already heading off the map. It was time to leave. Before he completely lost his head.

He took Simone's hand and helped her to her feet. "I'm afraid my father's locked me into some dreary Christmas function tomorrow night. Some promotional do for one of the companies he's trying to push me into. I don't suppose you'd like to come."

She laughed softly. "Now that's the most flattering invitation I've ever received. You make it sound very enticing."

He sent her a wry smile. "Well, to be honest, I'd rather not give my father the chance to leap to astronomical conclusions about you. About us."

"Oh? Well, thanks for the warning. I'll try to remember that if I ever run into him again." She squeezed his hand lightly. "Don't worry. My PA muttered something this afternoon about a corporate function I have to attend tomorrow night, so I'm already booked. Anyway, we can't see each other three nights in a row, Ryan. After all, we're supposed to be taking things one step at a time, aren't we?"

Yes, of course. It was worrying that he found it so difficult to remember that. He was going downhill fast. Simone Gray seemed to fill his every waking moment.

CHAPTER SEVEN

SITTING before her dressing table's mirror in a ruby silk dress that had cost far too much, Simone held up her mother's diamond and pearl drop earrings and turned her head from side to side as she admired their classic beauty.

They looked gorgeous and she needed something impressive for this evening's Christmas party. All of Sydney's top jewellers would be there. The place would be dripping with glamorous women and the combined value of the jewellery on display tonight could probably clear the national debt of a third world country.

But she wasn't sure that she should wear these very precious earrings tonight. They were the only expensive jewellery her mother had owned. Her grandfather had given them to Angela to wear when she'd married Douglas Gray.

Simone looked down at the creamy pearl drops shimmering softly in the palm of her hand and pictured her mother slipping the fine gold wires through her ears as she dressed for her wedding, her heart full of excitement and hope for her life ahead.

Thanks heavens she hadn't known…

Simone sighed heavily. She probably shouldn't wear these earrings, shouldn't think about her mother tonight. She would get too worked up and she needed to be cool and relaxed—charming, smooth and witty—at her corporate best.

But perhaps the pearl drops had cast a spell on her. Almost as if guided by a ghostly hand, she opened the drawer in her dressing table and took out the framed photo of her parents. Her eyes misted as she saw the very attractive, laughing young girl, arm in arm with her tall, fair and handsome, very young husband in his army uniform.

She stared at the image of her father and tried to imagine how it must have been for him to be sent off to war at the age of nineteen. Never to return. What had he been like? His face looked a little serious. Who could blame him for that? But there was a light in his eyes that suggested a sense of humour. Had he been excited when he'd learned that she'd been conceived?

She longed to have met him.

Longed to be able to talk to her mother. Just once would do.

If only she could talk to someone about her family. It had been great to let off steam with Belle and Claire on the mountain top, but that night felt unreal now, as if she'd dreamed it. If she never talked about her parents again, she might burst.

She tried to imagine telling Ryan—telling him everything. Saw the horror on his face and, without warning, tears spilled down her cheeks.

No! She mustn't cry. She'd already done her make-up.

But she couldn't help it. Tears fell heavily as memories of her mother washed over her—the warm comfort of her mother's loving arms, her mother's light, happy voice reading stories at bedtime and singing hit tunes from the seventies slightly off-key as she did her housework. Her mother's hands, slim and cool and gentle, applying lotion when she had chicken pox, bringing her dry crackers and flat lemonade when she had an upset tummy, a hot-water bottle when her periods had started.

But then the bad memories came—everything else that had happened later swept over Simone in a dark, rushing flood. All the horror. The guilt.

She mustn't, mustn't think about that.

The earrings fell on to a cut glass tray and Simone jumped to her feet. She unzipped her dress with shaking fingers. Sick and frantic, she hurried to the bathroom. She had to wash her face and start all over on her make-up. Which meant she would be late for the party.

And wouldn't her Managing Director be pleased about that?

Ryan glared at the marble floors and mirrored walls of the enormous ballroom and ran an irritated finger around the inside of his uncomfortably stiff collar. He couldn't believe he'd actually let the old man talk him into coming to this function tonight. Sucking up to his father's business associates was his least favourite pastime.

But it was a trade-off. If Ryan attended this party tonight JD was prepared to excuse him from the traditional Tanner five-course Christmas dinner.

It had seemed fair enough. Ryan was glad to escape the family gathering which always highlighted, in excruciating juxtaposition, his brother's outstanding successes and his own black sheep failures.

He was used to doing deals like this with his dad. Everything in JD's life was negotiated. His apparent generosity always came with a price tag.

But tonight, as Ryan surveyed the array of businessmen in penguin suits and women in glittering evening gowns, he could not, for the life of him, think why the old man had wanted him here. JD hadn't introduced him to one prospective employer, hadn't lined him up with one prospective wife, had paid him almost no attention, actually.

It didn't make sense. But at least it meant Ryan could sample the free food and drinks and slip away early, unscathed.

He helped himself to another beer, selected a canapé from the offerings on a silver platter and popped it in his mouth.

"Ryan, what are *you* doing here?"

He spun around and almost choked on his smoked salmon and cucumber.

Simone.

She was wearing a stunning dark red dress and her hair was caught up in a tiny feathered clasp, leaving her neck and shoulders bare. Tiny ruby-red gemstones sparkled in her earlobes. She looked sensational. He couldn't breathe.

All around them, male heads were turning to gawp at her.

"Fancy seeing you here," she said, smiling straight at him and ignoring her admirers.

Her blue eyes, made dramatic by mascara and kohl, regarded him with such open delight, that his heart performed back flips.

"I thought you had to go to a function organised by your father," she said.

"I did. This is it."

"Really?"

Ryan swallowed.

"Well, well." Her face turned pink with pleasure. "How nice. We get to see each other tonight, after all. I must say you scrub up rather well." She let her eyes rove over him with sparkling approval.

He felt fifteen and star struck. All he wanted to do was stare at her, couldn't speak, couldn't prise his tongue from the roof of his mouth.

"There you are, Simone!"

A voice to their right made them both turn. A rather corpulent red-faced fellow in his fifties rushed forward and embraced Simone. "I've been keeping an eye out for you. Where have you been hiding? I was beginning to worry that you weren't coming."

To Ryan's surprise, she looked suddenly discomposed. "Arthur," she said quickly, dropping a peck on the fellow's flushed cheek. "I'm sorry I'm late. Something unavoidable. Let me introduce you two. Arthur, this is Ryan Tanner. Ryan, Arthur Howard is our company's Managing Director."

"Tanner?" Arthur Howard pumped Ryan's hand with astonishing vigour. "You're not Jordan Tanner's son, are you?"

"I am," Ryan admitted without enthusiasm.

Arthur's face grew animated. "That's fortunate." He turned to Simone. "Did your PA pass on the message? JD insisted that you must be here tonight."

"Well, no. She stressed that it was important, but I thought this function was to launch a new line of jewellery."

"It is. Jordan Tanner's value adding to the output of his mines." Arthur chuckled. "That guy doesn't miss a trick."

Simone's eyes widened and she shot a sharp, puzzled glance to Ryan. "I didn't make the connection."

Ryan felt his stomach fall.

"And Tanner's considering *City Girl* for a huge advertising campaign," Arthur explained.

Like hell, thought Ryan.

"How wonderful," said Simone.

Ryan's teeth clenched as he bit back a retort. Now it was all falling into place. JD's insistence that he be here tonight was a set-up. His father had taken one look at Simone at his flat the other night and had decided to interfere, to try his hand once again at blatant and embarrassing matchmaking. But Ryan was damned if he'd let him. If he won Simone, he wanted to do it totally on his own.

Quickly, he scanned the room and saw JD in the corner. Ostensibly he was chatting to a group of businessmen, but his eyes kept wandering, darting this way.

A waiter with a tray of drinks approached Simone and she selected champagne.

Ryan, watching over her head, saw, to his dismay, that JD was excusing himself from his group and was crossing the room. Towards them.

Bloody hell. Fury billowed through him like black smoke through a chimney. He wasn't going to stand around while JD interfered in his life. Again.

If only he could take Simone aside and warn her about his father's subterfuge, but her Managing Director was in deep, animated conversation with her. He could hardly drag her away. And JD was zooming across the room like a heat-seeking missile.

If he stayed and had it out with JD he'd create a public spectacle.

Ryan dipped his head in Arthur Howard's direction. "It's a pleasure to meet you, sir," he said coolly. "I hope you enjoy the rest of this evening." He nodded to Simone. "Nice chatting with you, Ms Gray."

Her mouth formed a surprised O and she stared at him, clearly confused by his sudden formality.

JD was close behind her now. Over her head Ryan's gaze locked with his father's. Two stags about to butt antlers.

"Make sure you encourage my father to spend a great deal of money on those advertisements," Ryan said as soon as JD was within hearing, and then he took a step backwards. "I need to speak to a man about a— a goldmine."

He heard Simone's surprised gasp as he turned away from her and he felt like a heel of the worst order, but he couldn't hang around to be the puppet in JD's manipulations. He kept walking. And he didn't look back.

"Simone, I can't believe you're going to kill Ryan Tanner's bachelor story."

Simone looked up from her desk and winced as she saw Cate storming into her office. After Ryan's bewildering behaviour last night, she wasn't in the mood to discuss him with her staff.

"The piece you wrote about him was fabulous," Cate declared. "And Karin did a brilliant job with his photo. You've got to go ahead with his story, Simone."

Simone shook her head.

"But why? What happened? Did Tanner threaten you with a lawsuit?"

"Of course not," Simone snapped. "Mr Tanner and I had a very civilised meeting. And I agreed to respect his privacy. But it's OK. I struck a better deal with Jordan Tanner, his father. A feature spread about interesting, colourful women who design jewellery with Australian gold and gemstones in their own homes."

Cate gave her a bemused smile, then shrugged. "Well, I guess if it's all settled, you won't change your mind. I've got a rally car driver that I suppose we can run as this month's bachelor. But he'll be a poor substitute for Ryan."

"Nonsense." Simone rolled her eyes and dismissed her journalist with a shooing gesture and was relieved that she managed to keep her expression neutral until the girl left the room. Then she let out a deep sigh and felt her face collapse.

She hadn't realised how far her feelings for Ryan had blossomed until last night. She'd been over the moon when she'd seen him at the party. He'd looked so handsome in his dark tuxedo—by far the most gorgeous man in the room—and she'd been so overcome, had felt so suddenly smitten by him that she'd almost expected violins to start playing.

But they'd hardly exchanged more than a handful of words before Ryan had become strange and cold and then disappeared completely.

To say that it had been a bad moment was an understatement.

After she'd gone home last night she'd lain awake, worrying about what it meant. Common sense told her that Ryan's issues with his father were behind the way he'd dashed off, but her insecurities threw up other possibilities. And somewhere in the dark, early hours of this morning she'd reached the alarming conclusion that Ryan had been embarrassed to be seen with her in public.

And hot on the heels of that thought had come a shaft of panicky dread. Had Ryan looked up old newspaper files and uncovered the story of her mother's trial? Had he decided he didn't want to have anything to do with a woman with such a murky family history?

The arrival of daylight had not allayed her qualms. She'd been on tenterhooks all morning.

Her desk phone rang and she jumped.

"Mr Tanner is here," said her PA. "Do you have time to see him?"

Simone's insides felt suddenly weightless, as if she'd stepped off a cliff. "Which one?"

"I beg your pardon?"

"Which Mr Tanner? The father or the son?"

"Oh." There was a breathless little laugh on the other end of the line. "This is definitely the son."

"Right." Simone's mouth went dry, her palms damp.

Was Ryan here to explain his behaviour? Or to tell her that it was all over between them, that he was no longer interested in getting to know her, slowly or otherwise?

"Shall I send him through, Simone?"

"Um—" Simone reached for the glass of water on her desk "—yes," she said and the glass shook as she took a sip. "But give me a minute. I—I'm just finishing something."

She reached for a tissue and blotted the beads of perspiration above her lip. Her heart thumped as she took a small compact from her top drawer and powdered her nose, tweaked her hair, freshened her lipstick. Ridiculously, she thought of Henry VIII's wives, proudly making sure they looked their dignified best before they laid their heads on the chopping block.

The intercom on her desk beeped. "Mr Tanner is coming through now," came the warning.

The compact clattered noisily as Simone dropped it in the drawer.

"Knock, knock."

She heard Ryan's voice and looked up as he walked into her office, dressed once more in his habitual jeans and T-shirt. He was smiling. What did that mean? Her heart thumped harder.

"Hi," she managed.

"How are you this morning?"

"I'm fine," she lied without quite meeting his gaze. "Please take a seat."

Ryan did so and then, before he could ask, she said, "I had a wonderful time last night."

"Glad to hear it."

"Your father was charming."

This was greeted by silence and a black look. She felt ill, but compelled to keep talking.

"We're very excited about all the business your father's sending our way." Carefully she lined up the pens on her desk as if her future depended on having them straight. "The new gold jewellery products are sure to be a hit. JD's aiming at the younger end of the market and I think that's a good—"

"Have you seen the colour of his money?"

"What?" Simone's head jerked up.

His face was twisted into an uncharacteristic sneer. "This wouldn't be the first time my father's made false promises as part of a matchmaking ploy."

"Matchmaking?" She stared at him, nonplussed. "Ryan, what are you talking about?"

"Didn't he make crass comments last night? About me? About us?"

"No. He talked with surprising insight about *City Girl* and its readership. Single women with purchasing power."

Ryan stared at her hard, then leaned forward, his gaze intent. "He didn't embarrass you?"

"No. On the contrary. As I said, your father was charming." *It was you who embarrassed me.*

Ryan ploughed agitated fingers through his hair. "I was so mad at him for setting us up last night."

Simone's bewilderment was turning to anger. Ryan had behaved abominably, but was blaming everyone else. She could feel her anger rising, like hot milk threatening to boil over. "Listen to what you're saying, Ryan. You're suggesting that the only reason your father placed these ads in *City Girl* is because of my connection to you. Do you really think this is all about you?"

Springing out of his chair, Ryan began to pace her office, glaring at the carpet.

"You've got to admit it's a coincidence. My father didn't know you from a bar of soap until he met you at my flat the other night."

"And is that your excuse for embarrassing me? For pretending not to know me and then disappearing?"

"You don't understand," he shouted, but then he came to an abrupt halt and his face went through a series of contortions as her words sank in. "I only did it to pull the rug from under my father."

"Well, thanks very much. And I was supposed to guess it was all theatrics on your part?"

He looked suddenly contrite. "I'm sorry, Simone. That's why I'm here now. To explain. You don't know this man like I do."

Strangely, her relief that Ryan still cared about her was lost in her concern for him. A worried frown drew his brows and his mouth down as he sank back into the chair.

Her heart melted. "Ryan," she said gently. "I know you won't want to hear this, but I think you're wrong about your father. About his business dealings with *City Girl*, at any rate. This is going to be a profitable business relationship between him and us. The ads have been pre-paid. It's all above board."

He sighed. "That's great, Simone. Milk it for whatever you can. But I still believe Dad's up to his usual tricks. Interfering in my private life."

"Ryan, he's your father. He obviously cares about

you very much." His bleak face prompted her to continue. "I never knew my father and I ended up with a monster instead. I'm sorry if this sounds like preaching but, from where I'm looking, you're jolly lucky."

He sat very still, staring at a spot on the floor, and then his gaze lifted and his smile was so little-boyish and cute she almost leapt out of her chair to hug him.

"I'm sorry," he said. "My behaviour last night must have been very confusing for you."

"Well, you can always make it up to me," she replied coyly.

Ryan grinned. "Are you free tonight?"

"Let me see." She tried to keep a straight face as she made a business of consulting her desk diary, but her mouth kept twitching into a delighted smile. "Actually, yes."

"Can I tempt you to dinner? Or a movie? Both?"

"That sounds lovely." Anything with Ryan would be lovely.

"Terrific." Ryan was on his feet. "I'd better get back to work."

"Me too."

She half expected that he might kiss her goodbye, but he sent her a cheeky wink that was so sexy she almost melted into a puddle on the office carpet.

In the doorway he paused. "I was wondering if Homer and David might like some surfing lessons over the weekend."

Her face broke into a huge grin, stretching from ear to ear. How could she have been mad at Ryan Tanner? He was the most gorgeous, caring, sensitive man. "I'm sure they'd love that. Will I send a message to Homer via the soup kitchen?"

"Sure. Let me know tonight."

He disappeared and, because she missed him already, Simone began to make notes beside the relevant slots in her desk diary.

> Friday: 7.30 p.m. *Dinner and a movie—RT*
> Saturday: 7.30 a.m. *Coogee Beach—RT +3.*
> Sunday: 7.30 a.m. *RT??*

A shadow fell over the page. Ryan was back beside her. She just had time to register the expression of dark intent on his face before he pulled her out of her chair and kissed her.

It was amazing. So unexpected. And in her office. Wonderful to be clasped against the solid strength of him, to have his lips locked with hers. Too brief, of course, but enough to cause a jolt in the middle of her chest that spread through her like an explosion.

"I'll see you later," he murmured. And then he was gone again.

Just like that.

Afterwards Simone sat very still for ages, touching her fingers to her lips, remembering the fierce, possessive pressure of Ryan's mouth against hers, thinking about what he'd said.

It was some time before the smile on her face faded. And then it was as if the sun had gone behind a cloud, as the awful worries that had haunted her during the night returned.

She had pushed those dark memories aside while she'd been talking to Ryan. But now that she was alone again, dread and guilt settled inside her, chilling her bones.

What on earth was she going to do? She and Ryan were supposed to be getting to know each other slowly. But she was rapidly falling in love with the man. Too fast. Too deep. Faster and deeper than anything she'd ever known before. And, if she knew anything about men, Ryan was rather keen on her too.

But if she wanted this to continue, if she wanted any chance of lasting happiness with Ryan, she was going to have to do something she'd never been able to do with any other man. She would have to tell him her terrible secret. It was only fair that he knew the truth about her.

Except…she didn't think she was brave enough, was too scared she might lose him.

How could she ever take such an enormous risk?

CHAPTER EIGHT

SITTING beside Simone on the beach and listening to the ceaseless crash and boom of the surf, Ryan wondered if he'd ever felt happier.

His life was on a roll again…things were better for him than they'd been in ages…

He and Simone had enjoyed a perfect date last night and they'd spent the whole of today at this beach with Homer, David and Pink. They'd surfed till they dropped. They'd dined, picnic-style, making their happy way through a mountain of crispy fried fish and salty potato chips drizzled with lemon and eaten straight from the paper. And they'd washed their feast down with bottles of cold lemon fizz.

There'd been lots of laughter. Everyone, even the ultra-reserved Homer, had shared stories. True stories, tall tales, jokes…

Now the kids were playing with an old semi-deflated football.

"They should sleep well tonight," Simone said, as she sat with her head nestled against Ryan's shoulder, watching them. "I hope they stay safe."

Ryan caressed her cheek with his jaw. "Don't worry about them. They'll be OK." He heard the edgy insistence in his voice and realised he was trying to convince himself.

For a moment they sat in silence, watching the surging ocean turn dark as the light faded.

"I must admit I keep remembering that horror story Pink told us about her family last Christmas," he said. "All those drunken adults screaming and fighting. Poor kid; she tried to make it sound funny."

"It was horrendous." Simone shuddered, and he wondered if she was remembering something from her own past that disturbed her.

Something to do with the business she never talked about?

Would she ever trust him enough to tell him about her family's secret?

"They make me feel quite motherly," Simone said, watching Homer tackle David. She chuckled as both boys tumbled on to the sand. "I want to gather them under my wing and tuck them into soft, clean beds." She sighed. "Trouble is, it's hard to know how far you should go when you try to help them."

"Homer's so proud of his ability to look after himself. All three of them are fiercely independent. Too much help and you'd dint their pride."

"You're probably right. If you offered to take them in, I doubt they'd accept."

"There's a fine line between helping and interfering." Ryan stiffened. Had those words come out of *his* mouth? He thought of JD and shifted restlessly.

Simone pulled out of his arms and watched him for a moment or two, her lovely eyes soft and contemplative. "Ryan, it's not too late."

A cold tension wound in his stomach. "What are you talking about?" But he knew, even before she answered.

"Your father."

Ryan swallowed. "What do you mean? That I'm as proud and stubborn as Homer?"

"Not quite."

"But you're making the point that I see my father's help as interference."

"Well, you do, don't you?"

"But that's because it *is* interference."

"Well meaning interference."

"That's debatable," Ryan said, but without malice.

If he was honest, he had to admit that his attitude to JD had toned down a notch or two since the conversation in Simone's office yesterday.

Maybe it was the tail wagging the dog, but the truth was—he wanted this woman. And she didn't like his habitual stubbornness and conflict with his old man. So maybe…he should try to do something about it.

He'd been thinking about a time a few years back when his father had extended an olive branch. JD had offered to sit down with him, to discuss his hopes as a father, and he'd invited Ryan to be open and frank about what he wanted to do with his life.

Ryan knew that he should have grabbed that opportunity, but at the time he'd seen it as yet another example of his father's interference.

"It's a bloody waste of time," he had shouted at JD as he'd walked away. But he'd looked back and he'd seen the hurt in his father's eyes. *Would never forget it.*

"Ryan, don't make the same mistake I made. I waited too long to talk to my grandfather. There's something I really, desperately need to tell him, but I've left it so late that he won't see me now. You mustn't let that happen with your father. You should make peace with him."

"I'd rather make love with you."

Simone laughed and hid her face against his shoulder. "The two aren't mutually exclusive."

He was silenced by a shaft of hot desire. All day he'd been taunted by her slim, lithe body clad in little more than a swimsuit. Not being able to touch her had been torture of the worst order.

She turned in his arms and pressed her lips to his stubbled jaw. "Is JD still in Sydney?"

"Yeah."

"Is he likely to be home tonight?"

Ryan sighed. "Oh, yeah. Dad's a creature of habit. Whenever he's in Sydney, he spends his Saturday afternoons sailing on the harbour and then he goes home to ring all his company managers for a weekly report. And for a really top finish, he watches old black and white movies till late."

"Why don't you go to him, then? He'll probably have finished sailing. Ring him up. Seize the moment. Make a start."

"Only if I can spend the night with you afterwards." His heart thudded heavily. Good grief, had he really just propositioned Simone?

"Ryan," she scolded in a breathless, husky voice. "I'm not a trading commodity."

"Of course you're not. But today's been fabulous and—and I want to spend as much time with you as I can." He drew her back into his arms and she melted against him. He kissed her.

"Hey, knock it off, you two," yelled Pink.

Talk about nervous!

As Simone walked into her apartment, her stomach was hollow and shivery, her chest tight and her heart was beating so fast she felt giddy.

So much to think about!

Had she done the right thing by sending Ryan to his father? Had she overreacted? What if they had an almighty row?

In terms of how those two men viewed each other, they were both obstinate and pig-headed. Unbending. Anything could happen.

But then, beyond that, was Ryan's unbearably exciting suggestion that he should spend the night with her. Oh, man…She'd hardly been able to tear her eyes from him today, watching the shift of his muscles as he'd held the surfboard steady for David, watching the sheen of water on his broad tanned shoulders.

But now, alone and waiting, she was pummelled by doubts. To make love with Ryan would be so much more than a communion of bodies. Her heart was involved.

And the more she got to know him, the more she understood that he was not simply a hot-looking surfer. He was sensitive, patient, funny and clever. But the more she liked him, the more she worried. She didn't want to hurt him.

She argued with her conscience:

I should tell Ryan everything. After all, I told Belle and Claire.

But what if it scares him off?

I should tell him anyhow. He sees me as some kind of superwoman, raising huge sums for charity, helping street kids, but he doesn't know the truth. What I've done.

If you tell him, you'll risk losing him.

I know. I know. I can't bear it.

She was such a hypocrite, lecturing Ryan about his father, when she couldn't tell him the truth about her past, had never been able to tell her own grandfather.

It was almost dark by the time Ryan reached his father's apartment, nestled on the Kirribilli foreshore, right on Sydney Harbour. His stomach churned as he pressed the doorbell. This was embarrassing. Crazy. Proof that he'd really lost his head over Simone. Her experiment would probably end in the mother of all brawls.

He heard footsteps coming through the house, too heavy to be the housekeeper's, and shoved his hands deep in his pockets as the door swung open.

JD stood there dressed in an ancient T-shirt, faded football shorts and very new-looking yachting shoes. His face paled when he saw his son. "Ryan! What is it? What's happened?"

"Nothing's happened. I just thought I'd drop in. Say hello."

JD's jaw dropped. His hand shook as he took off his spectacles, folded them and put them in his shirt pocket.

"Can I come in?" Ryan asked awkwardly.

"Yes. Yes, of course." JD stepped back and gestured for Ryan to enter. "This is a surprise."

Ryan steeled himself to face a barrage of questions, but JD said simply, "I was in the study. But come through to the kitchen. Would you like a beer?"

"Thank you."

His father seemed to be recovering from his initial shock. Colour was returning to his face. But, as Ryan followed him, he thought JD looked a little thinner, more stooped, realised that his old man was actually getting *old*.

"Pity you weren't able to stay the other night. You missed a good party," JD said, not quite meeting Ryan's gaze as he handed him his beer. "Interesting people." He selected a small bottle of soda water for himself.

"Yes, it was unfortunate that I couldn't stay. Pressing business."

They both knew Ryan was lying, but JD didn't comment. They went out on to the terrace where there were two hundred and seventy degree views of the harbour. Below, the lights of sailing boats, ferries and water taxis zigzagged on the silky water. Ryan looked across to the lights of Sydney Cove, the birthplace of Australia, and suddenly wanted to bring Simone here to share this amazing spectacle. Wished she was here now. He could do with a little barracking from the sidelines.

"I'm very impressed with your Simone Gray," his father said, as if reading his thoughts.

"She's not *mine*." Ryan tried to smile through gritted teeth and wondered if he should leave immediately.

JD was happily unaware of his tension. "You've got your eye on her, haven't you?"

Ryan sighed. "I'm sure half of Sydney—the male half, at least—have their eyes on Simone."

"You're dating her?"

"Listen, Dad, I didn't come here to talk about Simone."

"You'll have to play your cards very carefully if you want to hang on to that girl, Ryan."

Ryan took a deep swig of beer, set it down with excessive care and willed his temper to cool. "I don't want or need your advice on how to manage my girlfriends," he said evenly. "Or any other part of my life, for that matter."

JD ignored him. "I've had Simone checked out, Ryan. She's a good proposition. Successful. I'll be honest, in the corporate world she's streets ahead of those other canaries you've gone out with in the past. She'd make a damn fine daughter-in-law. But you'd need to lift your game if you hope to impress her."

Bloody hell. Ryan's jaw clenched hard enough to crack it. "Give it a miss, Dad. Tell me about the sailing today. Where'd you go?"

"Simone wouldn't be interested in a beach bum, son. The Tanner name on its own won't be enough to impress a girl of her calibre. You'll need something solid to back you up. You'll have to settle down. Show some mettle. Get a steady—"

"That's enough!"

Ryan leapt to his feet, about to walk out. Relented, with great reluctance. He'd promised Simone that he would give this a go. But she had no idea!

He stepped to the edge of the terrace, watched the rows of twin red tail-lights and white headlights heading to and away from the Harbour Bridge. He supposed he should tell JD that he was making a much better living than anyone realised, but for too long now he'd taken a secret delight in keeping his private investments under wraps.

"Seriously, son, you should try to lasso Simone Gray. I'd throw a grand wedding for you. No expense spared."

"That's very generous, Dad, but forget it."

"But aren't you keen on this girl?"

"That's the problem," Ryan muttered beneath his breath as he continued to stare at the view. "You're deluding yourself if you think I'd take advice from you on how to handle women."

"And you'd be a fool not to take my advice." JD chuckled. "I've persuaded three women to marry me."

Oh, yeah? And we all know why.

Where was Gloria, JD's third wife, now? In Monte Carlo, no doubt. Unable to tear herself from a casino table.

JD let out a noisy sigh. "I'm only thinking of what's best for you, Ryan."

Ah...There was the rub. If Simone were here, she'd tell him this was his cue...

Ryan slammed his palm on to the balcony railing. It was OK for Simone to hand out advice—she was looking at this from the outside. She hadn't lived his life.

Turning slowly, he walked back and resumed his seat. His father was sitting very straight, his arms folded defensively over his chest.

Leaning in to him, Ryan asked, "Why can't you ever trust me?"

This was met by silence.

Ryan's heart pumped fiercely.

JD's jaw squared and he pulled his arms more tightly across his chest, tucking his hands beneath his armpits.

"I haven't done one thing in my entire life that's pleased you, have I?" Ryan persisted.

"Of course you have."

"I haven't. I've never once had a chance. Because you've never forgiven me for my mother's death."

"Ryan!" JD's jaw dropped like a trapdoor. His arms fell limply to his sides and his entire body sagged as he gaped at his son. His eyes were as shocked and round as an owl's.

Bloody hell. He'd said it. The thing he'd been burning to say to his dad since he was nine years old.

But without warning, JD's strong face crumpled. The muscles in his throat and around his mouth worked fiercely. "That—that's not true, son."

To Ryan's horror he felt a rock the size of Sydney Harbour Bridge jam his throat. His eyes stung and his vision blurred.

He wasn't sure how long he sat there, numbly fighting tears, unable to look at his father's sunken figure. He was trapped by a cold, dark fog of despair, the despair he'd fought for as long as he could remember.

He was startled when he felt a strong hand grasp his shoulder. He looked up and saw JD standing beside him, his eyes glittering.

"I know I've been overly possessive, Ryan. I lost the love of my life when you were born." JD swallowed as if to gather strength before he continued "I've been terrified that I'd lose you as well. That would be too much for a father to bear."

A shocked sound, somewhere between a sob and a cry of triumph, broke from Ryan as he rose to his feet. He almost staggered under the weight of his emotion as his father threw his arms around him.

It was almost eleven o'clock before Simone accepted that Ryan had changed his mind, that he wouldn't be visiting her tonight.

She'd spent the first part of the evening in a flurry of nervous excitement, shampooing her hair, giving herself a pedicure and rubbing lotion into her legs. But then, when she should have relaxed on the sofa with a glass of wine, watching TV while waiting for Ryan, she'd begun to pace the apartment, worrying, watching the phone, watching the clock, willing Ryan to call.

What was keeping him? Had he and his father had an almighty row? Was Ryan mad at her?

At ten minutes to eleven, she gave in, made a cup of hot chocolate and took it up to bed. She doubted she would sleep, but she had a good book, a blockbuster thriller that she hoped might, just *might* hold her attention.

She climbed between the sheets, took a sip of hot

chocolate, opened the book and settled comfortably in the little pool of yellow light cast by her reading lamp.

The warm light reached almost to her dressing table, making her room cosy and safe. Her bottles of scent glinted and the cut glass bowl that held her mother's pearl drop earrings twinkled in the semi-darkness.

Simone's eyes began to droop. Gosh, she hadn't realised how exhausted she was after a day of sun and surf and a long anxious evening…

She woke with a terrible start, her heart pelting as if she'd run a mile. The phone was ringing. She sat up. The lamp was still on and her book had fallen to the floor.

She almost stumbled as she ran down the stairs to the kitchen, grabbed the receiver. "Hello?"

"Simone, it's Ryan."

Her heart continued a wild kind of tango. What time was it? What had happened? "Where are you?"

"At your front door."

Her front door? Why was he on the phone, then?

Still half asleep, she took a moment to understand, peered down the hallway to her tomato-red front door.

"I knocked," Ryan said. "But you didn't hear me. I'm sorry. I guess I've woken you up."

"No, no, it's OK. I'm coming." She hurried down the hall and flung the door open wide, pressed a hand against the sudden thudding in her chest.

The sight of Ryan on her doorstep made her head swim with a dizzying rush of happiness.

"I'm really sorry I'm so late. I hope you don't mind. You were asleep, weren't you?"

"It's OK. I don't mind. I dozed off. What's the time?"

"Almost midnight."

"I can't have been asleep for very long." She ran her hand through her sleep-tumbled hair and felt rather self-conscious to be standing in her doorway in her skimpy nightdress of thin blue silk. She stepped aside to let him in. "How did it go with your father?"

"Amazingly well, actually."

"Oh, Ryan, I'm so pleased."

"We had a lot to talk about and time got away. That's why I'm late."

"Have you eaten?"

"Dad and I made a huge pot of pasta."

"So you and your father got on *that* well?" she asked as he followed her down the hall. "Does that mean you've settled everything between you?"

"Well, you can't undo twenty years of misunderstanding overnight, but we've made some good progress." Ryan snagged her wrist, pulled her towards him and smiled so endearingly she almost cried. "And I have you to thank for it, you wonderful girl."

She felt the heat of his fingers encircling her wrists and swallowed nervously. Ryan mightn't think she was so wonderful if he knew *everything*.

"I'm so pleased it worked out," she said. "You look happy."

She could see it shining in his eyes.

"I brought something for you," he said. "Actually, Dad sent it, but I selected it, so I guess it's from both of us. It's part of the new collection that *City Girl* will be advertising."

From the pocket of his jeans, he drew out a necklace—

a fairy tale concoction of pink crystals, large and small, with fine gold chains and a darling gold dragonfly pendant. Simone loved it instantly.

"Ryan, it's gorgeous. How did you know I have a thing for dragonflies?"

"Lucky guess."

She shot him a shrewd look. "You remembered that article I wrote about the bike ride and the gorgeous dragonflies in China."

"Maybe I did," he admitted with a cute boyish smile. "Here, let me see how it looks on you."

The heat of his fingers brushed against her skin as he held the necklace around her throat.

"It looks perfect," he said. And then, more gently, "You're perfect, Simone."

Oh, dear. If only…

If only…

Simone didn't realise that she'd closed her eyes till she felt the warm, sensuous caress of Ryan's lips on the curve of her neck, on her bare shoulders. He touched his lips to her ear lobe and sent exquisite shivers skittering over her skin. She felt his fingertips beneath her chin and then, with the softest of groans, he turned her face up to his.

Oh, my!

Ryan. Right here. Wanting her…His face betraying a breathtaking tenderness…His lips trembling into a shaky smile…Dark heat flaring in his eyes.

His emotion and desire were so visible they caused an ache in her chest, made her feel like a goddess, made her want to lose herself in his warm, musky maleness.

He lowered his face, touched his lips to her lips, made her feel all woozy and melting, so that she had no choice but to surrender, to let her anxieties slide away into the night, couldn't think of anything but how much she wanted Ryan's kisses. Wanted his strong arms holding her, his hands caressing her.

She wanted skin contact, lots of skin contact. Wanted his mouth locked with hers, his hard strength deep within her. Wanted *him*.

His hands cupped her breasts. "Simone," he whispered gruffly. "Do you have any idea how lovely you are?" His thumbs grazed her through her silk nightdress, seducing her with slow, sensuous sweeps.

His mouth claimed her again, less gently. Then his hands caught her about the hips, pulling her deeper against himself.

The longing inside her flared, liquid and hot, driving low.

"Where's your bedroom?" he murmured.

"Upstairs. Too far away."

Her trembling knees couldn't take her all the way up there. The sofa would have to do. Or the kitchen counter, an arm chair. The floor. Anything. Anywhere, just as long as this wonderful feeling didn't stop.

But suddenly she realised that Ryan had scooped her up. He was carrying her effortlessly. Up the stairs.

Moments later, she was exceptionally grateful.

How heavenly it was to tumble together with him on to her big, comfy mattress, to be helped out of the nightdress. To help him out of his clothes. And at last! The bliss of total contact, of his silky, bronzed skin, smooth against hers, his hard male muscles wedded with her soft feminine curves.

"You are perfect," he breathed.

He was perfect too. The perfect lover. Tender, yet dominating. Passionate as he paid her body exquisite attention, his touch more ardent and sure, his kisses more arousing than any she'd ever known.

Pleasure engulfed her.

And she sought to give Ryan pleasure too, caressing and kissing him everywhere. Till finally he could wait no longer. He had to take control. Take her.

Ah…this was so right. She and Ryan were meant to be together.

Like this. Only this!

Yes!

It was afterwards, when Simone was lying beside Ryan, loose-limbed, blissed-out and coming back to earth from an all-time high, that her troubled thoughts crawled back like spidery ghosts.

It was like waking from a wonderful dream to discover that her real life was the nightmare. Dismay slammed into her with the force of a truck at high speed. She lay very still and tried to banish the thoughts.

If only she could delete parts of her life with the press of a button. Memory wiped clean.

"Simone, what is it?" Ryan took his weight on one elbow so he could study her face. "What's the matter?"

Unable to get the words out, she looked away, humbled by the tenderness in his eyes. She couldn't bear to tell him, couldn't bear to see his reaction when he heard her story.

His hand brushed a strand of hair from her cheek. "Bad memories?"

Sweat broke out all over her skin. Her mouth went dry.

"This is connected to your family and what you wrote in your diary, right?"

She nodded.

"Are you sure you don't want to talk about it?"

She tried to speak, but couldn't form the words, couldn't fight through the wall of sudden panic.

"Why don't I—I go and make us a cup of tea?" she offered lamely.

"Time for that later." With a hand beneath her chin, he drew her face closer. "If you're not going to tell me what's troubling you, you'll have to keep your mouth right here so I can kiss you again."

She tried to smile, but felt too nervous.

He kissed her lightly on the lips, scattered a warm, sensuous trail of kisses over her neck and shoulders until, once again, she began to relax.

"Do you want me to keep this up or do you want to talk?"

She wanted his kisses. She knew she should talk. *Oh, God.* "I should talk."

Ryan propped himself on one elbow and smiled at her, rubbed her arm gently. "Hey, don't look so worried."

"I'm worried about what you'll think of me."

"I'm not easily scared off, you know."

"I—I don't know how to tell you."

"Any way it comes."

"It's terrible, Ryan."

"Well…I'm not easily shocked either."

She remembered that Belle had said something similar on the fateful night in the Himalayas, when they'd all spilled their secrets.

Simone pictured herself up there on the mountain top, listening to Belle talk about her lost sister Daisy and her unhappy marriage with Ivo, hearing Claire confess about the way she'd mistreated Ethan. She remembered the strange, unreal courage she'd felt when it had been her turn…

Could she do it again?

Sitting up, she tried to ignore the frantic, fluttering wings of panic inside her. "It—it's about my mother."

Getting that out helped. She felt something shift inside her. A rusted hinge, creaking open?

"Hang on a sec," she said and she slipped out of bed and went to the drawer in her dressing table, brought back the photo of her parents and handed it to Ryan.

"These are my parents. Angela and Douglas Gray."

Ryan sat a little straighter and studied the photo while she got back into bed beside him and, dragging an aqua sheet under her chin, drew a deep breath.

"They look very nice," he said. "Very young."

"They were only nineteen. They were married just before my father went off to Vietnam."

"You look like them. You have the best of their features—your father's attractive colouring and your mother's lovely eyes and mouth."

She nodded and bit her lip.

Ryan put his arm around her shoulders and drew her

against the big, comforting wall of his chest. He kissed her cheek, very gently. "What is it? What happened?"

The air in the room seemed to close in, as if fog had crept under the windows and doors. Simone struggled to breathe. Panic threatened to wipe her out.

He set the photograph on the bedside table. "Let's rearrange these pillows and get more comfortable. And then you can tell me everything."

Tell him everything.

It was going to happen. She'd pushed herself to the point of no return. Sick to the stomach and shaking, she watched Ryan arrange her collection of aqua, deep blue and white pillows into a comfortable mound.

"Come here, gorgeous girl." He smiled and patted the space beside him and she knew there was no other place she would rather be.

If only she didn't have to talk…

He drew the sheet over them and his arms tightened about her. Once again, he tucked her head against his solid bare shoulder and he touched his warm lips to her forehead and the raw edges of her panic receded. Just a little.

"You've already told me that your father died in Vietnam," Ryan said. "Your mother must have been very young when he died. But you said you had a stepfather. When did she marry again?"

"When I was ten she married Harold Pearson."

"And you didn't like him?" He said this as if her dislike had been obvious in the tone of her voice.

"He was a monster of a man. I hated him. He was always drunk and he used to beat up my mother. You've no idea how awful it was. W-when I was fifteen, there was a terrible fight one night and—and Pearson fell down the stairs."

Just remembering that brought dread, like a dark menace, filling her with horror. She shuddered. "You don't need to hear all of this, Ryan. I really should go and make us a cup of tea."

She tried to slip out of bed, but Ryan caught her wrist. "Simone, tell me. There's more, isn't there? Something awful happened."

"Yes," she whispered and then she sighed. "He—he was killed."

"When he fell?"

"Yes."

His arms were around her once more, rocking her gently. "So, what happened?"

"There was a trial…They charged my mother. It was terrible, Ryan."

"You poor girl. They actually charged your mother?"

"The jury wouldn't wear murder. She was convicted for manslaughter."

A surprised gasp broke from him. "Convicted?"

Eyes closed, she nodded against his shoulder. "Mum was sentenced to five years, but she died. Only two years into her sentence."

"I'm so sorry, Simone." He hugged her close. "That's so unfair. On all counts." He dropped a kiss on to her forehead. "What happened to you?"

"Oh, I was OK. My aunt and uncle took me in. Aunt Edith is my father's sister. No, it was my mother who suffered."

"Five years sounds like a steep sentence for a woman struggling with a violent husband."

"It was totally unjust, Ryan. But—" Simone's mouth twisted down and she had to take a deep breath before she could go on. "You see, Mum didn't try to defend herself. She simply made a full admission. She wanted to get everything over as quickly as possible."

She shoved her hand hard against her mouth, wanted to howl, but knew she mustn't.

Ryan lifted a strand of hair from her cheek. "I can't imagine how terrible this must have been for you."

She closed her eyes as the harrowing memories crashed over her. She saw her mother's face as she'd stood in the witness box. Hard, so hard, not giving a single emotion away.

"Simone, this is a terrible thing to have happened, but it's all over now." Ryan took her gently by the shoulders. "You can't change the past, sweetheart. But you can try to put it all behind you."

Her eyes flashed open. Oh, dear heaven. Ryan thought it was finished, that she'd told him everything.

But she'd only just begun. She still hadn't told him the worst.

CHAPTER NINE

Too late, Ryan realized he'd cut Simone's story short, that whatever was troubling her had not been silenced. He was angry with himself for not sensing it earlier. He should have encouraged her to go on. To get *everything* out in the open.

But she wouldn't continue. She insisted instead that she needed a cup of tea and so, wrapped in kimonos, they went down to the kitchen.

Watching her hands shake as she filled the kettle and fetched mugs, Ryan felt helpless. Despairing. It wasn't fair that Simone should be so troubled.

She had done so much for him. He would be eternally grateful to her for sending him to visit his father this evening. But that couldn't compare with the joy of making love with her. Nothing in his experience had compared with that.

Simone was responsible for the incredible elation and sense of freedom that bubbled inside him. He wanted her to feel it too. But her terrible memories had come like ghosts to trouble their joy. Her joy.

He ached for her. She deserved happiness. He wanted to heap happiness on her.

He cursed himself for being so hasty, for assuming that her story was told. Had to find a way to help her.

His instincts were to keep his arms around her, to cradle her close, to shelter her with his body, to silence her fears with his lips. But no, this wasn't a time for kisses.

For now, he had to stop thinking about the taste of her mouth, the feel of her sensuous, feminine body, had to get her to start talking again.

They carried their mugs of hot tea to the sofa and he sat beside her, could feel her tension tight as a bowstring. She stared straight ahead, as if she was unable to look at him, and he waited till she'd almost finished her restorative drink before he spoke.

"Simone, there's something else you need to talk about, isn't there?"

She shook her head, drained her mug and set it down on the coffee table.

Ryan grazed her cheek with his knuckle. "Tell me," he commanded gently.

"I can't." She let her head fall against his shoulder and he tried to ignore the fragrant smell of her hair as it brushed his cheek.

"I guess it is very late," he admitted. "Maybe you should get some sleep. We can talk in the morning."

He expected her to jump at this chance to escape his questioning, was surprised when she said, "I want to tell you, Ryan, but I just can't get it out. It's too awful. I told Belle and Claire in the Himalayas. But I don't know how I did that now. I've never told anyone else. I—I haven't even been able to tell my grandfather."

"Is this the grandfather who won't speak to you?"

She nodded. "I promised Belle and Claire. We all made a pact and I pledged to come back to Sydney and go to my grandfather and tell him this—this—"

She sat up suddenly, but wouldn't look at him. Spoke to the opposite wall. "I wanted to confess. To—to get my grandfather's absolution. But I've been avoiding him for years—and now he won't have anything to do with me." She swallowed. "I can't really blame him. It's all my fault. I don't know what I'm going to do."

"But you feel that you have to tell him this, don't you? That your happiness depends on it?"

"Yes…But—" She covered her face with her hands, then let them fall. She sighed. "I don't seem to be able to put it behind me. I suppose I could write him a letter and hope that he reads it."

"But that might not work. It would be better if you talked to him."

"I know." Her face was a picture of defeat.

Ryan took her hand in his, kissed it. "You know there's an obvious solution."

"If only there was, Ryan."

"You'll have to front up to your grandfather and refuse to leave until he hears what you need to tell him."

She paled. "I couldn't."

"You can, Simone." He squeezed her hand tightly. "You know you have to, don't you?"

She shook her head. Her free hand fluttered in a gesture of helplessness. "How could I tell him if he doesn't want to see me? What would I do? Set up camp on my grandfather's veranda? Lie across his doorstep? Make him have to step over me if he wants to leave Murrawinni?"

"I'm sure that won't be necessary. Once he actually comes face to face with you again, he'll relent."

"I wish I could believe you, Ryan." After a bit, her mouth tilted into a wry smile. "Does this conversation have a familiar ring to it?"

"How do you mean?"

"It feels like an echo. Only a matter of hours ago we were on the beach and I was bossing you around, telling you to go to your father."

"The best order I've ever been given." He tucked a wing of silky golden hair behind her ear. "And now you should take your own advice."

"But I'm not as brave as you."

What she didn't say, he realised, was that her problem was far more serious than his. The death of her stepfather, the death of her mother in jail, were grave matters. His impatience with his father was a molehill compared to the mountain of cares that burdened Simone. And it seemed that this other thing that still troubled her was even bigger.

"I'll go with you," he said with sudden certainty. "To your grandfather's. We'll tackle this together."

At first she didn't respond. She sat very still, staring at the floor. "I couldn't ask you to do that."

"You don't have to. I've already offered."

"But it's too much to expect of you, Ryan. I shouldn't

have dumped all this on you. After all, we haven't really known each other very long."

His face broke into a brief grin. "Haven't we? I must have known you in a past life, then. I feel as if I've known you for ages."

Her blue eyes shimmered as she turned to him. "Would you really come? Seriously?"

"Seriously, Simone; I'm insisting that I come. And I won't listen to any arguments."

She sat very still, taking this in.

He sensed the moment she made her decision, felt the sudden tension in her and the answering release. It came and went quickly, no more than the vibration of an archer's bow when an arrow was shot.

She turned to him again and he could see hope burning in her eyes. "Ryan, that would be wonderful. When should we go?"

"You're the boss. Why don't you take time off work, so we can head out there tomorrow?"

She nodded, her face glowing with sudden excitement. "I think I might actually be able to do it if you came too."

Taking his face between her hands, she kissed him happily. And Ryan returned her kiss, pouring everything into it, wanting to share with her all the new and wonderful happiness bubbling inside him…Her gift to him. Lightness of spirit. Hope. Love…

It had all seemed so possible when she'd been talking to Ryan in her apartment, but Simone's confidence deserted her as she opened the white post and rail gate for Ryan to drive his Jeep on to her grandfather's property.

Everything about Murrawinni was sadly familiar— the gentle hills covered in a blue eucalyptus haze, the long winding track across tree studded paddocks, the wide, silky river, the dam where kangaroos gathered at dusk.

A port wine magnolia still stood in front of the house, a white crepe myrtle at the side. And the house was as beautiful as ever—an old colonial brick homestead with two magnificent bay windows in front and a low, wide veranda wrapped around it.

It was like stepping back in time, straight back to the golden days of her childhood.

If only…

As Ryan pulled up on the gravel drive to the side of the house, a pair of sheepdogs came rushing up to them, leaping about the vehicle and barking madly.

"Oh, heck," Simone muttered. "This is a great start."

She was a mess of nerves, felt sick as she picked up her handbag and slipped its strap over her shoulder.

Ryan gave her a smile and a wink. "I know what you're going through. I wanted to turn tail and run for the hills rather than set my foot on my father's front doorstep. But just remember I'm right here beside you. And I'll still be beside you when this is over."

She nodded and gave him a grateful smile. Felt a leap of guilt. Poor Ryan had no idea what he was getting into here.

At least, as they got out of the Jeep, the dogs stopped barking. Simply came close and sniffed and wagged their tails.

"See?" said Ryan. "They're house dogs, not guard dogs."

He took her hand and together they crossed the sunburnt lawn, past the tinkling fountain to the front steps, climbed them and crossed the veranda to the big, glass-panelled front door.

Simone half expected that Ryan would take charge, but he stepped back and gestured for her to knock.

There was a small old-fashioned bell beside the door. Her palms were sweaty as she pulled the chain.

Ryan dropped a swift kiss on her cheek as they waited.

And waited.

"There's no one home," she said and felt a guilty twinge of relief. "Let's go, then. I'll have to do this by letter after all."

"Hang on, Simone. I can hear someone coming."

He was right. There were footsteps, sometimes muffled by carpet, sometimes striking the timber floor.

At last the door opened and there stood her grandfather, looking frighteningly old and frail, but in other ways just as Simone remembered, dressed in neatly pressed trousers and a long-sleeved shirt and woollen tie. His hair had turned silky white years ago, but he was handsome still, rugged and lean, his eyes as deep, smoky blue as the distant hills.

Grandfather. She tried to speak, but her throat was too choked.

"Can I help you?" he asked in his refined elderly baritone, so instantly familiar to Simone that she had to fight a sudden rush of tears.

Jonathan Daintree looked from Ryan to her. Looked

again, more sharply. "Simone?" His voice trembled. "What are you doing here?"

"Hello, Grandfather."

It was the moment she'd longed for. The moment she'd dreaded. But now that she was face to face with this man who'd been such a wonderful grandfather, the man who'd stepped into the role of her father, she was awash with happy memories. They gathered about her like a warm embrace.

She glanced quickly at Ryan, caught his smile. Felt a quiet confidence stir within her. "I need to talk to you, Grandfather. Can we come in?"

He didn't answer at first and she remembered her manners. "Sorry. Introductions first. Grandfather, I'd like you to meet Ryan. Ryan Tanner."

Ryan extended his hand and the two men shook.

Jonathan Daintree's eyes narrowed as he turned stiffly to Simone. "Well, you've come a long way. This must be important. I guess you'd better come in."

"Thank you."

Her mouth was dry as they followed him into the house, down a central hallway to the lounge room, an elegant, high-ceilinged room with classic curtains and wallpaper, brushbox floors and antique oriental rugs.

Just inside the room, Jonathan stopped and speared Ryan with an acutely curious look. "Are you any relation to the infamous JD Tanner?"

"Yes, sir, I'm his son."

The old man studied Ryan. Intensely. Up and down.

Oh, dear, thought Simone and the wings of panic returned. What had JD done to upset her grandfather?

"Interesting fellow, your father. When I was in politics he sent me a letter telling me that every one of my policies was wrong and downright stupid."

Simone blanched. Slipped to the edge of real despair.

But Ryan smiled calmly. "That sounds exactly like my father."

Jonathan's face twisted into a wry smile. "Interesting man indeed," he said, nodding while his smile flickered a little longer.

But when he returned his attention to Simone, his face sobered. "Please, take a seat."

Simone was grateful that Ryan sat beside her on the deep tapestry-upholstered sofa. She was grateful for the solid warmth of him, remembered his words:

I'm right here beside you. And I'll still be beside you when this is over.

She slipped her hand inside his.

Her grandfather sat opposite them. "Well, Simone, I'm sure you understand you're the last person I expected to see out here."

He'd never been one for beating about the bush. He liked to get straight to the point.

"I assume I can speak frankly in front of Mr Tanner," he said. "You've avoided contact with me for years."

She opened her mouth, but her grandfather kept talking.

"I'm not silly, Simone. I know when I'm being side-lined and pushed away. For years the doors to Murrawinni were open to you to come whenever you wanted.'

Simone nodded sadly. "I'm sorry we've drifted apart. It's my fault entirely."

This seemed to surprise him. He studied her for a moment. "I felt there was something troubling you," he said less sternly. "But you were always too busy to talk."

"I know. I've been avoiding you. And I've felt terrible about it, Grandfather. I—I hope you'll understand. You see—it—it was all about a promise to Mum."

His face paled. "Angela made you promise never to see me again? To avoid me?"

"No, not exactly. But there was something Mum made me promise not to tell you. And I knew that if I saw you it would come out somehow."

His mouth trembled. "But you're going to tell me now?"

She nodded again, suddenly too nervous and upset to speak.

She *had* to do it. She had to tackle this immediately. Her grandfather was not the kind of man who would want to sit around having cups of tea and talking about the weather before getting to the reason for her visit.

She glanced quickly at Ryan beside her, read reassurance in his eyes and decided there was nothing for it but to dive in. "It's to do with Harold Pearson. And the trial. And—and Mum."

Jonathan didn't move.

"There's something that didn't come out at the trial," Simone said and a lurch of fear churned her stomach.

Ryan reached for her hand. *Thank you.* She sought courage and strength from the warmth of his touch. Found it. *I love you, Ryan.*

She said quickly, "It should have been me."

Her grandfather stared at her, his lack of comprehension clear in his puzzled eyes. He looked at Ryan. "Has she told you about this?"

"No, sir." Ryan stroked the back of her hand with his thumb. His warm brown eyes met hers. "What do you mean, Simone?"

Oh, heavens. This was it. She had to say the words.

"My mother shouldn't have gone to jail. It should have been me."

Jonathan leaned forward, his eyes searching hers. "Why do you think that?"

She couldn't tell him.

Ryan looked worried. "Simone?"

She simply couldn't get it out.

"Were you there?" Ryan asked gently. "On the night Pearson died?"

"Yes!" She flinched as the single word broke from her. Turned her head so neither man could see her face. "I did it."

She felt the sudden tension in the room. It was like a live thing. Pulsing. Suffocating her. Awful. Far worse than she'd ever imagined.

Her chin trembled alarmingly, but she knew she couldn't back down now. "I was the one who pushed Harold Pearson. I was trying to stop him from hurting Mum, trying to get between them, and I shoved him aside and—and he was drunk and he lost his balance and—and fell down the stairs."

"Simone."

"Oh, sweetheart."

The shocking words jerked out of her. "I killed him."

With a hand pressed against her agonised mouth,

she turned to catch Ryan's response. Not horror, as she'd feared, but deep, stark sorrow. She looked at her grandfather and saw her own raw pain reflected in his eyes. It cut her to her core.

But now she'd started she felt compelled to get it all out. Her horrible story spewed from her in a high-pitched nervous stream. Bullets from a machine gun.

"Mum wouldn't let me confess. She told the police that *she* pushed Harold. She insisted and, no matter how hard I tried to stop her, she wouldn't listen. She wouldn't let me give evidence. M-mum lied in court and went to jail instead of me."

Her mouth pulled out of shape with the effort of holding back tears. "And—and—I did what she told me. I let her go."

"Of course you did, you poor girl. You were only fifteen, only a child." Jonathan looked shaken, but his voice was steady. "You didn't have a choice. You were a victim."

She swiped blindly at her eyes. "Mum always tried to protect me. She didn't want my life tainted by Pearson. But she shouldn't have gone to jail. She shouldn't have had to die in the prison hospital. They said her illness was aggravated by stress."

She wanted Ryan's arms around her, couldn't bear the worried look on his face, but couldn't hold back.

"It was my fault Mum died. I killed her."

"No, you didn't," Ryan protested.

"I did. It was my fault."

"If anyone's to blame, it's that brutal stepfather who made your lives a misery."

"But I killed him too," she wailed.

"But you were defending Angela." This time it was her grandfather's voice. "It was an accident."

A groan broke from Ryan. It frightened her. She couldn't look at him. What did he think of her? Was he horrified?

Deep inside she felt something give way—perhaps the barred door that she'd kept tightly locked for so long.

Too long.

Sadness and loss flooded her and burst up into her throat. A howl broke from her and she collapsed on to the sofa in a wild fit of sobbing, was engulfed by such deep despair that she had no choice but give in to it.

Her whole body heaved as huge, painful, hacking sobs tore from her. She couldn't help it. Kept crying even when her throat ached from an excess of tears. She couldn't stop.

She wanted her mother back.

She wanted her mother, her soldier father. Life was so hard without them. She had tried to right her wrong, had worked hard at her studies, had striven to reach the top of her career, to prove to the world that she wasn't an evil person, but what was the point?

What was the point?

What was the point of anything?

Simone wasn't sure how much time passed before she discovered, with some surprise, that her sobbing had slowed.

"Simone…" her grandfather's voice sounded, somewhere above her "…Simone, my poor child."

A hand patted her head gently and she looked up to find him leaning over her, his eyes gleaming damply.

She struggled to sit up. Felt her throat burn and swiped at her eyes with the back of her hand.

It was only then that she realised that there was space beside her where Ryan had sat. Her heart rocked. Had her confession been too much for him? "Where's Ryan?"

"I wanted a little time alone with you. He went off to the kitchen."

Her grandfather sat beside her in the place Ryan had vacated, put an arm around her trembling shoulders.

"Can—can you ever f-forgive me?" Her voice sounded strange, tear-ravaged.

"Forgive you, Simone? I'm the one who should ask *you* for forgiveness. We adults let you down. All of us. That sod, Pearson, and—and Angela. As for me, I—I just wish—" He shook his head sadly. "I tried to help Angela. I arranged for the best QC in the country to take up her case, but she wouldn't have anything to do with him."

"Mum panicked, I think. She was frightened that a clever lawyer could force her to tell the truth. He would have wanted to know *exactly* what happened. She was—was trying to protect me."

"Yes." Jonathan sighed heavily. "If only Angela had confided in me, I could have told her that they would never have convicted you, Simone. It was an accident. It would have been very easy to prove. Neither of you needed to suffer."

In a rational corner of her mind, Simone had known

this for years now, but it had never seemed to help her to feel any better. The futility of her mother's sacrifice was almost as hard to bear as her own horrible sense of guilt.

Raising a shaky hand, her grandfather adjusted his spectacles. "Angela was always headstrong. She wouldn't listen when I tried to warn her about Pearson. I was at my wits' end when she rushed off and married him."

Jonathan closed his eyes and Simone could see his distress in the tightly drawn, downward curving line of his mouth. She hugged him hard. "I'm sorry to land this on you after all this time."

"I'm very grateful that you did, my dear." He smiled at her. "I have my little Simone back."

"Oh, Grandpa." She clung to him and he held her close. She could smell the clean, laundered cotton of his shirt, could feel the beating of his heart through his frail chest, could feel tears on his cheeks. And on hers.

Could feel the horrible weight inside her begin to ease.

At last...

At long, long, last...

They talked for some time...about her parents, about her childhood, about life...

And, while they talked, Simone felt reconnected again in a way she hadn't felt since she'd left Murrawinni at the age of ten. She felt as if she'd been given her life back.

CHAPTER TEN

RYAN sat in a squatter's chair on Murrawinni's side veranda, looked out over the long stretch of paddocks that ran down to the river and heard JD's warnings echo and rattle in his head. Marbles in a tin can.

Simone wouldn't be interested in a beach bum, son. The Tanner name on its own won't be enough to impress a girl of her calibre. You'll need something solid to back you up.

It had been water off a drake's back.

Till now.

Now Ryan had heard Simone's story and he knew his father spoke the truth. Simone had coped with so much, with horrific liabilities, had dealt bravely with huge issues—horrendous, real life baggage that would have broken a weaker woman.

She'd achieved so much too. She'd managed to get on with her life. Alone. She'd held down an extremely responsible position at *City Girl*, raised shed-loads of corporate donations by cycling through the Himalayas, and she cared about street kids. Heck, she didn't just care about them. She got off her cute butt and did something constructive.

By comparison, Ryan knew he'd had minor problems—issues with his father, a chip on his shoulder that most guys shed in their teens. And yet he'd allowed these relatively minor annoyances to cripple him.

Slumping forward, elbows on knees, head clasped in his hands, he stared bleakly at the pale biscuit-coloured paddocks of grazing sheep. What did he have to offer Simone? He could write, sure. He could sell his freelance stories without much trouble, but he'd never tried to forge a career. Found plenty of excuses to drift.

He'd been fooling himself that his life was OK. That he was the kind of guy Simone might be interested in spending her life with. Hell, he realised now he'd never looked in the mirror and seen the real Ryan Tanner, the aimless rolling stone without ambition or means. The drifter his father and the rest of the world saw.

It was a manifestly discomfiting thought.

After Simone washed her face and brushed her hair, she went in search of Ryan and found him on the veranda, sitting alone, looking pensive. And rather pale, despite his tan.

He rose as she approached and his eyes shimmered as she reached to take his hands in hers and lifted her face for a kiss.

"Thank you so much for bringing me here," she said. "I couldn't have spoken to my grandfather without you."

"My pleasure. Did you and Jonathan have a good chat?"

"Yes. He's been great. I feel such a wonderful sense of being able to let go. I feel better about everything."

"Happy?"

"Very. Happier than I've felt in a long, long time. Too long. Even better than I felt after I confessed to Belle and Claire."

"You deserve to be happy," he said as he wrapped his arms around her and held her.

But Simone sensed that something was different about Ryan. His embrace felt wonderful, but there was something missing in his voice, in his eyes. Her heart teetered out of kilter. Had he been totally horrified by her story?

It was completely understandable that a man might not want to tie himself to a woman with such a dark background. Did Ryan wish to distance himself from her now?

She pulled away, looked into his face. "Ryan, are you OK?"

"Of course. I'm really happy for you."

"I'm sorry I dumped such a huge mountain of my emotional baggage on you," she said. "You probably think I'm ready for the loony bin."

"Nonsense. I think you're amazingly sane. The most together woman I've ever met."

She wanted to believe him, but there was still something in his eyes, a caution that she'd never seen before. It frightened her.

Her grandfather insisted that they stay the night. "Connie's already made up the guest room for you, Ryan.

And you can have your old bedroom, Simone." Jonathan's blue eyes twinkled. "I hope that arrangement suits you both."

They both assured him that separate rooms were perfectly fine.

But Simone felt an embarrassing blush heat her face. She glanced at Ryan, but his expression was neutral and she couldn't tell what he was thinking.

Connie, her grandfather's housekeeper, could, apparently, perform miracles. That evening she prepared a fabulous meal—a hearty, three-course country-style celebration befitting the return of Jonathan Daintree's prodigal granddaughter.

Jonathan was in high spirits, more than happy to play the jovial host, which was fortunate—if it weren't for him, the conversation over dinner would have been rather flat. Ryan joined in, but from Simone's perspective he seemed to be growing more reserved by the minute.

Or, Simone wondered, was she expecting too much of him? After all, they hadn't known each other terribly long and the poor man had been dragged headlong into her personal maelstrom.

"Did you know you're very much like your father, Simone?" Jonathan asked, interrupting her thoughts as he topped their wineglasses.

"Do you think I look like him?"

"You have his colouring, but it's more your character. He was quite a hero."

Surprised but pleased, she set down her knife and fork, eager to hear more. "Was he really? In what way?"

"He died in Vietnam, right at the end of the war, trying to pull a wounded mate away from enemy fire." Her grandfather reached for her hand and gave it a squeeze. "You have that same courage, my dear. I'm not at all surprised that you tried to protect your mother."

"That's a lovely thing to say."

"It's the truth."

She glanced at Ryan and he raised his glass to her. "I agree with your grandfather. You've lot to be proud of, Simone."

He smiled but, to her dismay, the smile didn't erase the shadowy *something* in his eyes, the disturbing light that had been there ever since she'd unburdened her confession.

She was rather relieved when the conversation moved on and she was asked to recount her trip to the Himalayas. She was happy to talk about the mountain villages and cities with their narrow cobbled streets and stone-lined streams full of goldfish, about bartering at the markets in the old city of Lijang and watching the Naxi people perform a traditional dance in the town square.

Talking about China led to talking about Hong Kong, which Jonathan had visited often.

"Have either of you been to the Temple Street night markets in Kowloon?" he asked.

"I have," said Ryan. "I found them fascinating. So many stalls that just appear at night. Clothing galore, Cantonese opera, pavement dentists and doctors."

Simone smiled. "And fortune-tellers."

Ryan's eyes widened. "Did you go to one?"

"I did, actually. I found this quaint little old man who had tiny birds in cages that hopped out to select envelopes with people's fortunes inside."

He grinned—a flash of the old Ryan. "I think I remember seeing something like that. A group of people huddled around, waiting very patiently for the bird to make its selection."

"Yes, it's all very intense and serious."

"But worth the wait?"

"Oh, I suppose so." Simone sipped some wine and smiled.

"Well, come on, what did your fortune reveal?" her grandfather demanded. "You can't keep us in suspense."

"Oh, it was just a bit of fun, really. It was written in Chinese, of course, so I had to find someone who could translate it for me."

"And?"

"I was told that something unexpected would happen. Something that would bring me great happiness, but it would come from an unlikely source."

As she told them that a shiver ran through Simone. She thought about everything that had happened since she'd returned to Australia—meeting Ryan, falling in love with him, his insistence that she come here, her grandfather's blessing at last.

Oh, my gosh, it's happened...I've come to Murrawinni and I've found the happiness I longed for. And Ryan is my unexpected, unlikely source.

She opened her mouth to share this with them, but Ryan's tight, guarded expression stilled the words on her lips.

He was frowning at her. "That's an obscure fortune, isn't it?"

It wasn't obscure. It was all very clear to Simone. Why hadn't Ryan made the connection?

She tried to make light of it. "As I said, Ryan, it was just a bit of fun. I'll probably work out what it means by the time I'm ninety."

"So how long have you two been together?"

The sudden question from her grandfather surprised them both.

"Ryan's a very good friend," Simone said quickly. "I wouldn't be here if it wasn't for his help."

But it seemed that Ryan felt a compulsion to be deadly accurate.

"Actually, sir, we only met a short time ago." He didn't look at Simone.

"Oh, I see," said her grandfather, as if he was seeing rather a lot.

A cold wind crept around Simone's heart.

After they went to bed, Simone lay awake. After they went to bed, Simone lay awake, exhausted but unable to sleep. She kept thinking of Ryan in the bedroom across the corridor. Was he asleep or lying awake too? Was he missing her as much as she missed him?

She couldn't believe how miserable she felt. Perhaps she was overtired and emotionally wrung out, reading things into Ryan's behaviour that weren't there.

It was unreasonable of her to be disappointed simply because Ryan had become a little standoffish and reserved in her grandfather's house. Most guys were probably nervous when they met a girl's family.

She thought about tiptoeing across the passage to his room. Her grandfather slept at the other end of the house, so no one would know. She wanted to feel his arms around her, needed his reassurance that everything was OK.

But his reserve had rattled her. Perhaps it would be best to let him sleep. And she should try to get plenty of sleep herself. Everything would be fine tomorrow. She and Ryan would be able to talk everything through on the trip back to Sydney.

If only she could sleep.

To Simone's dismay, Ryan steered their conversation to street kids on the journey home. He suddenly wanted to tell her about research he'd done on the Internet. He was terribly excited by a scheme that offered credit to street kids to help them to start their own small business.

"I've been thinking that if David and Homer had bicycles they could start up a courier business," he said. "Kids on bikes can be incredibly quick because they don't get held up in traffic jams."

Simone knew it was a wonderful idea and she told him so, but she didn't want to talk about Homer and David and Pink right now. She wanted to talk about them. Was disappointed that Ryan was making it diffi-cult for her.

She was getting more frightened all the time. Now that she'd finally offloaded her secret, had her worst nightmare come true? Was the man she loved pushing her away?

Of course the fact that she was terribly tired didn't help her mood. She'd lain awake all night, too keyed up by everything that had happened. Memories and thoughts had played tag in her head—her childhood at Murrawinni, her mother…Ryan…

If only she'd slept…She could hardly keep her eyes open now…

"Hey, sleepyhead, we're almost home."

Simone struggled to sit up and discovered that she'd been sleeping at an awkward angle, her head hanging sideways like a rag doll's, and now her neck was cramped.

Ryan smiled at her. "You've been out like a light for hours."

She still felt dazed as he drove through the familiar streets of her suburb. As he pulled up outside her apartment he said, "Will you be going to work tomorrow?"

"Yes, I have to. You know what deadlines are like." She yawned. "But I feel like I could sleep for a week."

"You need an early night."

"Please, come up and have coffee."

He smiled gently, leaned across and kissed her. "You're out on your feet. I'll catch up with you tomorrow."

No. She didn't want Ryan to leave now. She needed to talk, needed *him*.

But she forced herself to be sensible, to put herself in Ryan's shoes. Perhaps he needed space—a little distance. The past few days had been rather intense and she supposed she wouldn't be very good company tonight.

"Ryan, thank you so much for coming with me to Murrawinni. Thanks for *everything*."

He caught her chin and held her close while he kissed

her. It was a friendly kiss, warm but without his usual passion. "See you soon," he said.

"Sure."

She was used to being alone, but as Simone watched Ryan drive away she realised it was true what people said—there was a world of difference between being alone and being lonely.

There was a fine layer of dust over all the horizontal surfaces in Ryan's flat and dead frangipanis lay scattered over the table like dried and blackened insects. They'd lain there ever since the night Simone had come to dinner.

He remembered Simone sitting at this table, sitting opposite him in the candlelight, looking divine. A goddess.

He tried to shrug off a sense of desolation, collected up the flowery corpses, tossed them in the rubbish bin, caught a faint whiff of their lingering scent as he did so.

Already he missed her.

Man, you've got it bad. You're a mess.

It had all seemed so easy that night at dinner. They were a man and a woman attracted to each other. Hey presto. Nature would take its course.

But he was so much wiser now.

So much more deeply in love. So much more afraid. Afraid that he'd rushed Simone. Afraid he wasn't worthy of her. His father's words came back to haunt him again.

...to impress a girl of her caliber. You'll need some-

thing solid to back you up. You'll have to settle down. Show some mettle.

JD was right. Ryan hadn't given his old man enough credit in the past. Simone's grandfather had acknowledged as much.

When they'd been leaving, Jonathan had taken Ryan aside.

"I mentioned yesterday that your father sent me a scathing letter, pointing out the errors of my way as a politician," he said. "But what I didn't tell you was that JD included a cheque, for a substantial amount, as a donation to my campaign funds. Said he admired passion and determination and he thought I was the only one in my party who had any fight in him." Jonathan chucked. "There's more to your father than meets the eye."

Ryan knew this was true. It was time to bite the bullet, to talk to his accountant and do something constructive with that money his mother had left him.

But was it too late to impress Simone?

Thing was, he and Simone had met under tense circumstances. They'd been through a complex and emotional journey together and rational judgement could be swept aside by heightened emotions. She was attracted to him, sure, and right now she was grateful for his help, but could she really want a future with him?

Ryan's phone was ringing when he got back to his flat late the next afternoon. He grabbed it just before it rang out.

"Ryan, mate. It's on. The big one. There's a one in a

hundred year storm in the Southern Ocean off the coast of South Africa. It's sending out wave patterns that will hit the sea mount off Tasmania. You know what that means."

"The mother of all waves." Ryan felt his pulse race. "How long have we got, Mick?"

"Less than twenty-four hours. I've got a big chopper with plenty of sea range on standby at Hobart. We've lined up a cameraman and a still photographer and there's one seat left for a scribe. You want to write about possibly the biggest wave anyone has seen in our lifetime?"

Within the hour, Ryan was packed and ready. He tried to ring Simone's office but she was tied up, so he left a message with her PA and another on her home phone. As the taxi pulled up outside his flat, he remembered to check his mailbox.

Lucky he'd remembered. There was rather a large packet in there and the box could have filled to over-flowing while he was away.

He didn't have time to go back into the house, so he brought the packet with him. He would shove it into his overnight bag later, but for now he held it as the taxi took off. Wondered what it was, why it felt vaguely familiar.

Halfway to the airport, curiosity got the better of him and he ripped the packet open. Fine hairs stood on the back of his neck as he saw the contents. A small book. With a brown leather cover.

Simone's diary.

His heart trembled as he took it out. She'd sent him her diary, her intimate secrets. It hadn't come by post, so she must have called past on the off chance of finding him at home and had put it in his mailbox. She wanted him to read it.

His throat constricted and his hand began to shake as he opened it and began to read.

Day One: Arrived in Bangkok at 10.30 p.m. Very hot and muggy. Tomorrow I enter China and I'm freaking out...

"You want domestic or international?"

Ryan looked up and blinked at the cab driver.

"Which terminal, mate? Domestic or international?"

"Ah—domestic, thanks," Ryan managed as he dragged his mind from his deep absorption in Simone's journal.

He closed the book, tried to gather his thoughts, to focus on the task ahead. Getting to Tasmania. Covering the story of a lifetime.

Like an automaton he paid his fare, went to the computer and punched his flight details to get his boarding pass. He put the diary in his bag while he went through Security, took it out again and continued reading when he found the right departure lounge.

It was all there in her book...Simone's fears and hopes, her deepest longings and secrets. The adventure of her journey, her delight in meeting Belle and Claire. And then her deepening conviction that she had to go home and lay the ghosts of her past. The final night when the three women made their pact.

Ryan picked up his reading pace, blocking the airport noise from his mind.

"Attention, calling all passengers boarding Flight 460 for Hobart…"

The announcement broke his concentration for a scant split-second. Ryan stood up to join the passenger queue, still holding the diary in one hand and reading. Then he stopped, totally absorbed by the next entry.

Suddenly it was as if Simone was there beside him, speaking softly into his ear, revealing the true secret of her diary…

It was all very well to tell my secrets to two strangers on a mountain top. The real test will come if I ever fall in love. Will I ever be able to tell that man what I've told Belle and Claire?

I have this happy dream in my head that one day I'll meet a man I can totally trust and I'll be able to tell him everything.

It would be a huge burden for him to have to take my story on board, but if it didn't frighten him away, if he still loved me in spite of my past, what a wonderful gift he would give me.

I know that if I'm ever able to tell him this it will be because I love him deeply and trust him completely.

Is it too much to hope such a man exists?

Is he out there somewhere?

I sit here at the top of the world and imagine I can see all the people on earth down below. Six billion. I only want just one.

One man I can share this diary with. Just one man who will accept me, my life, my heart.

CHAPTER ELEVEN

SIMONE couldn't believe how disappointed she felt. She'd arrived home from work to discover a message from Ryan on her answering machine. He'd gone to Tasmania.

Tasmania?

What about her diary?

It could remain sitting in his mailbox for days! She'd taken it to his flat during her lunch break, hoping to catch him at home, had needed to see him, to reassure herself that she'd been imagining that troubled, distanced light in his eyes.

She'd agonised over the decision all morning at work, but decided she had to do it. She was sure that Ryan was the one man in the world for her. She loved him, couldn't begin to imagine her life without him.

And she was so worried that the story she'd told her grandfather had upset Ryan. That was why she'd wanted him to read her diary, wanted him to see the full picture, wanted him to know that she was able to put the past behind her now. And she wanted him to understand exactly how important his help had been. What it meant to her.

But he'd gone to Tasmania.

It was ridiculous really. If only she could laugh.

Without changing out of the red suit and high heels she'd worn to work, she hurried back down to her car, garaged in the basement. It was still peak hour and she hated driving at this time of day, especially now when she was worked up and shaky. Heartsick. But she couldn't leave the diary sitting in Ryan's mailbox until he got back.

She reversed her car out and there was a blast of a horn as she almost ran into a flashy BMW convertible that was backing out from a bay behind her. Slamming on the brakes, she jerked her car forward, out of the sports car's way. Wanted to cry with frustration.

Get a grip, girl.

Once the other car left, she reversed again, this time making it out of the car park without mishap, and she emerged on to the street, only to have to brake again to avoid a pedestrian dashing across the road.

Zap!

A lightning-like jolt hit her as she recognised the pedestrian. It was Ryan.

Ryan, looking every kind of gorgeous in blue jeans and a long-sleeved navy shirt. Ryan on the footpath now, waving to her.

Why wasn't he in Tasmania?

There was another blast of a car horn behind her. *Oh, heavens.* Here she was, sitting in her car in the middle of the road, holding up traffic, while she gaped at Ryan. She sent him a frantic wave and drove off down the street, had to continue on for a block before she could turn around and come back.

She parked in the street, got out, a picture of confusion.

But Ryan was smiling. Laughing. Running to her. He swept her into his arms and held her tightly against him, as if he couldn't bear to ever let her go.

"What happened?" she cried, her head spinning with bewilderment and joy. "I thought you were in Tasmania."

"I've read it, Simone. I've read every word. I was just about to board the aircraft and I read the final entry in your diary and I had to come back."

Ryan set her down, but she felt as if she was still in the air. Her heart was a balloon, taking off for the stratosphere. "I wanted you to know everything, Ryan. You're the one person in the world I wanted to have no secrets from."

"You have no idea what that means to me, Simone. I just couldn't get back here quickly enough."

"But I didn't want to upset all your plans. Weren't you going to see the ultimate wave? The one you've always wanted to report?"

"Forget about Tasmania, darling. I can wait another hundred years for the next one. This is more important."

"What is?"

He took her hands in his. "Us. I'm your one man in six billion, remember?"

"Oh, Ryan." She wanted to laugh and cry. "I've been panicking about whether I did the right thing."

"It was the perfect thing...the sweetest thing."

"I've been so worried about you."

"Why?"

"The story I told my grandfather seemed to upset you.

You've been different ever since we went to Murrawinni, Ryan. Troubled."

"Not because of your story."

"What, then?"

He lifted a strand of her hair, wound it lightly around his finger. "I was humbled by how brilliantly you've coped with everything, Simone." He released the curl. "You've had this terrible emotional burden for years but you've still got on with your life and reached the pinnacle of a business career. You are a truly remarkable woman and I started to think I was a poor match for you."

"A poor match? Are you joking? You're a perfect match, Ryan."

"But I'm just a part time writer and a beach bum, as my father has so kindly pointed out."

"You're not a beach bum." Simone stared at him, totally shocked. "You're the most exciting man I've ever met."

"I don't even have a proper career plan."

"I don't want a man with a proper career plan. I can't love a career plan. A career plan can't make me feel the way you do, Ryan. I want you, Ryan Tanner, just as you are. There is nothing about you I want to change."

His eyes sparkled as he grinned at her. "But I do intend to make some changes. I've got trust fund investments that I've tried to ignore. If I did come up with a proper career plan, would you object?"

"I—" She paused to give this thought. "I don't suppose so. Not if you choose something you enjoy." A disturbing thought struck. "But I hope this doesn't mean you're going to give up surfing."

Ryan laughed. "No chance of that. I still have plans for us to hit the beach and I'm not going to sell my surfboard. But you might have to get used to seeing me in a business suit more often."

"I'd rather see you in nothing but a towel."

He chuckled sexily.

"Although I can cope with business suits," she decided. "Actually, I believe you'd look rather dashing in a double-breasted pinstripe suit."

"I have lots of plans that I want to run past you. If you like, we can make those decisions together. You might even want to get involved."

"You bet; I insist on being involved. What kind of plans?"

Ryan smiled again and his gorgeous, dark brown eyes shone very brightly. "Well…my first plan is to tell you that I love you, my darling girl."

"Oh, Ryan."

Simone didn't care about the traffic rushing past; she kissed Ryan in full view, right where they were standing in the middle of the footpath.

"You know you're the man of my dreams."

With gentle fingers he traced the curve of her ear. "My next plan is to ask if you would do me the incredible honour of becoming my wife."

Happy tears gathered in her eyes.

"And the mother of my children."

Too overcome to speak, she nodded ecstatically.

"We can have a good life, Simone."

"Yes, a wonderful life."

Happy beyond words, Simone threw her arms

around Ryan and kissed him long and hard. A horn blasted behind them and they both turned to see an elderly woman in a passing car grinning madly as she gave them a cheery thumbs up.

Ryan and Simone laughed, waved back, but then they grabbed hands and hurried inside, out of view, up the stairs.

They had a lot to discuss…among other things…

EPILOGUE

"THIS isn't the way to your father's. Where are you taking me, Ryan?"

They were supposed to be meeting with JD to discuss Ryan's decision to buy into a chain of outdoor and leisure magazines.

At least that was where Simone thought they were heading, but Ryan was driving in the wrong direction, to the northern suburbs.

"Won't we be late?"

He grinned at her. "Don't worry, Simone. I warned Dad we might be a little delayed. I wanted to show you something first. I have a surprise for you."

"A surprise?" Her life seemed to be full of wonderful surprises these days. Right now, she was in the midst of exciting wedding plans.

"We're nearly there," Ryan said. "Close your eyes."

She obeyed, feeling as puzzled and excited as a child playing blind man's bluff.

The car made a turn, then slowed to a stop.

"OK." Ryan kissed her cheek. "You can open your eyes now, my darling."

My darling... How utterly blissful that sounded. Simone was grinning as she opened her eyes.

They were parked in the front driveway of a house—a very appealing sprawling house in a pretty tree-lined street. It looked like a family home with glass doors opening on to a pergola-covered courtyard and a magnificent old jacaranda tree in the middle of the front lawn and—

Simone gasped. "Oh, my goodness." She turned to Ryan, saw his look of heart-stopping tenderness. "It's—it's just like the dream house in my diary, isn't it?"

He grinned, took some keys from his pocket. "Come and see what you think."

She was laughing and crying as she darted ecstatically from room to room. The house had *everything*.

"There's an island bench in the kitchen," she exclaimed.

"To encourage family togetherness," Ryan quoted from her diary.

"And there's a lovely paved barbecue area in the back yard. And another pergola covered in flowering vines." Simone grabbed his hand. "Oh, Ryan, there's even a swing hanging from a tree in the backyard."

She counted the bedrooms. Four. Bathrooms—two. A family room, an office, a sunken lounge, a dining room big enough for Christmas and birthday parties, a large garage, a shady garden...

It was her dream home, even more perfect because it wasn't brand-new. She was quite certain she could feel the happy vibes of the family that had lived here and loved here, had left a blessing.

"Oh, Ryan. You darling, darling man." She hugged him hard and he lifted her high, spinning her in happy circles. Joyful tears streamed down her cheeks. "How on earth did you find it?" she asked when he set her down again.

"I've been looking every chance I had, ever since I read your diary."

"It's perfect."

"I know."

"I can't believe you remembered every detail."

"It was easy, darling girl. It's my dream home too."

Was it possible for a girl to be any happier?

Well, yes, it was possible...Simone discovered twelve days later, when she saw the joy and pride in Jonathan Daintree's eyes.

"You look absolutely radiant, my dear," he said.

Simone laughed. "I feel as if I'm glowing all over today." She slipped her arm through her grandfather's and dropped a kiss on his cheek, careful not to smear him with her lipstick. "I must say, you look rather suave."

He was dressed in a dinner suit with a black bow-tie and was standing as tall and proud as his ageing spine would allow.

Simone had chosen a simple white wedding gown and she wore her mother's pearl drop earrings, carried frangipanis and wore them in her hair.

"We all look amazing." Pink grinned, so excited and nervous she could hardly stand still.

She had burst into tears when Simone had asked her to be a bridesmaid.

"I like to think of you as my surrogate little sister," Simone had explained to her. "So you're the perfect choice to be one of my bridesmaids."

And because Ryan had already bought Homer and David bicycles and helped the boys to set up their courier business, which was doing well enough for them to move into shared accommodation, Pink hadn't needed too much persuading.

Cate from *City Girl* was the other bridesmaid and today both Pink and Cate looked perfectly lovely in gowns of the palest sea green chiffon, with deep pink frangipani in their hair and in their bouquets. Simone had insisted on frangipani to remind her of her first date with Ryan—the dinner at his flat.

Belle had sent beautiful English roses, which would add to the glamour of the wedding reception, along with the magnums of champagne from Claire.

Now, from beyond a small grove of trees, the sweet strains of a flute and harp floated to them. It was almost time.

"If Homer and David laugh at me, I'll kill them," Pink muttered.

"They wouldn't dare to laugh," Simone reassured her.

"They'll be struck dumb by how pretty you look," said Jonathan and Pink blushed and looked prettier than ever.

Cate announced, "OK, no more talk. They've started our music." She was the one member of the wedding party who didn't appear nervous. "It's time for us to get going. Remember, you lead, Pink."

Jonathan secured Simone's arm more firmly in his.

"You have no idea how thrilled I am to be able to give you away to your wonderful young man," he whispered.

Simone smiled at him. "I think Mum and Dad are watching somewhere," she whispered back.

"They are, my dear. I'm sure of it."

They shared another smile tinged with sad memories, but full of love and brimming with promises for the future.

And then grandfather and granddaughter set off, following Pink and Cate down the short stretch of winding pathway flanked by trees and flowering shrubs till they emerged on to a grassy terraced headland overlooking the long sandy curve of Palm Beach and, beyond that, the dazzling blue of the sea.

Everyone was here—Simone's aunt and uncle, JD and Gloria, Ryan's brother and his wife, the rest of the *City Girl* crew and select friends, including Homer and David. Everyone was rising from their seats and turning to greet the bride with misty-eyed smiles.

And then…at the front of the gathering, three men were standing to one side.

Simone saw Ryan, her wonderful bridegroom, looking achingly gorgeous in a black dinner suit with a crisp white shirt, his handsome face alight with love and smiling at her.

Only at her…

The musicians played the last chords and the celebrant beamed genially over the assembled guests as Simone took her place beside Ryan…

She looked up and her bridegroom smiled into her

eyes, smiled beautifully, just as he had the very first time she had seen him waiting in the airport taxi queue.

Here was her perfect match…her one man in six billion…to have and to hold…for ever.

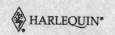

EVERLASTING LOVE™

Every great love has a story to tell™

*An uplifting story of love and survival
that spans generations.*

Hayden MacNulty and Brian Conway
both lived on Briar Hill Road their whole
lives. As children they were destined to
meet, but as a couple Hayden and Brian
have much to overcome before romance
ultimately flourishes.

Look for

The House on

Briar Hill Road

by award-winning author
Holly Jacobs

Available October wherever you buy books.

www.eHarlequin.com

HEL65419

HARLEQUIN®
Super Romance®

Welcome to our newest miniseries, about five
poker players and the women who love them!

Texas Hold'em

When it comes to love, the stakes are high

Beginning October 2007 with

THE BABY GAMBLE

by USA TODAY *bestselling author*

Tara Taylor Quinn

#1446

Desperate to have a baby, Annie Kincaid
turns to the only man she trusts, her ex-husband,
Blake Smith, and asks him to father her child.

Also watch for:

BETTING ON SANTA *by Debra Salonen* November 2007
GOING FOR BROKE *by Linda Style* December 2007
DEAL ME IN *by Cynthia Thomason* January 2008
TEXAS BLUFF *by Linda Warren* February 2008

Look for THE BABY GAMBLE *by* USA TODAY
bestselling author Tara Taylor Quinn.

Available October 2007 wherever you buy books.

Silhouette®

Romantic
SUSPENSE

**Sparked by Danger,
Fueled by Passion.**

When evidence is found that Mallory Dawes
intends to sell the personal financial information
of government employees to "the Russian,"
OMEGA engages undercover agent Cutter Smith.
Tailing her all the way to France, Cutter is
fighting a growing attraction to Mallory while at
the same time having to determine her connection
to "the Russian." Is Mallory really the mouse in
this game of cat and mouse?

Look for

Stranded with a Spy

by *USA TODAY* bestselling author

Merline Lovelace

October 2007.

Also available October wherever you buy books:

BULLETPROOF MARRIAGE *(Mission: Impassioned)*
by Karen Whiddon

A HERO'S REDEMPTION *(Haven)* by Suzanne McMinn

TOUCHED BY FIRE by Elizabeth Sinclair

REQUEST YOUR FREE BOOKS!
2 FREE NOVELS PLUS 2
FREE GIFTS!

HARLEQUIN ROMANCE®

From the Heart, For the Heart

YES! Please send me 2 FREE Harlequin Romance® novels and my 2 FREE gifts. After receiving them, if I don't wish to receive any more books, I can return the shipping statement marked "cancel." If I don't cancel, I will receive 4 brand-new novels every month and be billed just $3.57 per book in the U.S., or $4.05 per book in Canada, plus 25¢ shipping and handling per book and applicable taxes, if any*. That's a savings of over 15% off the cover price! I understand that accepting the 2 free books and gifts places me under no obligation to buy anything. I can always return a shipment and cancel at any time. Even if I never buy another book from Harlequin, the two free books and gifts are mine to keep forever.

114 HDN EEV7 314 HDN EEWK

Name	(PLEASE PRINT)
Address	Apt.
City	State/Prov.	Zip/Postal Code

Signature (if under 18, a parent or guardian must sign)

Mail to the Harlequin Reader Service®:
IN U.S.A.: P.O. Box 1867, Buffalo, NY 14240-1867
IN CANADA: P.O. Box 609, Fort Erie, Ontario L2A 5X3

Not valid to current Harlequin Romance subscribers.

Want to try two free books from another line?
Call 1-800-873-8635 or visit www.morefreebooks.com.

* Terms and prices subject to change without notice. NY residents add applicable sales tax. Canadian residents will be charged applicable provincial taxes and GST. This offer is limited to one order per household. All orders subject to approval. Credit or debit balances in a customer's account(s) may be offset by any other outstanding balance owed by or to the customer. Please allow 4 to 6 weeks for delivery.

Your Privacy: Harlequin is committed to protecting your privacy. Our Privacy Policy is available online at www.eHarlequin.com or upon request from the Reader Service. From time to time we make our lists of customers available to reputable firms who may have a product or service of interest to you. If you would prefer we not share your name and address, please check here. ☐

HR07

HARLEQUIN®

Mediterranean
NIGHTS™

*Sail aboard the luxurious Alexandra's Dream and
experience glamour, romance, mystery and revenge!*

Coming in October 2007...

AN AFFAIR TO
REMEMBER

by

Karen Kendall

When Captain Nikolas Pappas first fell in love with
Helena Stamos, he was a penniless deckhand and she
was the daughter of a shipping magnate. But he's
never forgiven himself for the way he left her—and
fifteen years later, he's determined to win her back.

Though the attraction is still there, Helena is hesitant
to get involved. Nick left her once...what's to stop
him from doing it again?

www.eHarlequin.com

HM38964

Coming Next Month

**Join us in elegant France, stylish Italy
and the rugged Australian mountains! Whether she's having the
boss's baby or being rescued by a millionaire, let Harlequin Romance®
take you from laughter to tears and back again!**

#3979 THE DUKE'S BABY Rebecca Winters

Join gorgeous but scarred Lance, Duc du Lac, in his majestic French
château. He wants nothing more than to hold a child in his arms and be
called "Daddy." Then he meets Andrea, who is pregnant, widowed and
alone....

#3980 THE MEDITERRANEAN REBEL'S BRIDE Lucy Gordon
The Rinucci Brothers

Join Polly on her trip to beautiful Italy as she gives Italian playboy Ruggiero
the news that he's become a father. Can she tame this wild Italian's heart?
Another one of the Rinucci brothers is about to meet his match!

#3981 HER PREGNANCY SURPRISE Susan Meier
Baby on Board

Hardworking Grace never expected to be pregnant with her brooding boss's
child. But in this beautiful story, find out how an unexpected little miracle can
help two people become a loving family of three.

#3982 FOUND: HER LONG-LOST HUSBAND Jackie Braun
Secrets We Keep

It's always hard to admit to your mistakes. Claire has never forgotten her
short-lived marriage to gorgeous Ethan. She sets out to find him and maybe,
just maybe, change their lives forever. Don't miss the last book of the
magnificent Secrets We Keep trilogy.

#3983 THEIR CHRISTMAS WISH COME TRUE Cara Colter

If you love Christmastime and just can't wait for the season to begin, then
don't miss the beautifully heartwarming story of Michael, a man facing his
first Christmas alone. When he volunteers to wrap children's gifts, he meets
Kirsten under the mistletoe....

#3984 MILLIONAIRE TO THE RESCUE Ally Blake
Heart to Heart

If you've ever wanted to be rescued by a knight in shining armor, then this
story is for you. Daniel sweeps brokenhearted and penniless Brooke away to
his luxurious mountain estate. This is one happily ever after you won't want
to miss.